"Just get me out of here...please."

Alisha's car was mere inches away from what looked like a sizable drop-off into a ravine.

"I've got you," Nathan said. "C'mon, take my hand."

She nodded. "My bag."

"Okay, grab it. But careful."

She lifted the big businesslike leather bag and handed it to him.

"Turn slowly toward me, okay?"

She nodded, the car rocking with each movement and slipping another inch against the old tree trunk.

Nathan's breath caught. That old stump wouldn't last much longer.

"On three," he said. "One, two...*three.*"

He tugged her up and out and then pulled her away from the now-shaking car. With a groan, the car's front right fender scraped against the rock before sliding over the edge of the ravine and crashing down below.

The sound of metal breaking apart echoed out over the hills.

"Are you all right?"

Alisha let out a long, shuddering sigh. "I could have died if you hadn't come along..."

With over seventy books published and millions in print, **Lenora Worth** writes award-winning romance and romantic suspense. Three of her books finaled in the ACFW Carol Awards, and her Love Inspired Suspense novel *Body of Evidence* became a *New York Times* bestseller. Her novella in *Mistletoe Kisses* made her a *USA TODAY* bestselling author. Lenora goes on adventures with her retired husband, Don, and enjoys reading, baking and shopping... especially shoe shopping.

Books by Lenora Worth

Love Inspired Suspense

Undercover Memories
Amish Christmas Hideaway

True Blue K-9 Unit

Deep Undercover

Military K-9 Unit

Rescue Operation

Classified K-9 Unit

Tracker
Classified K-9 Unit Christmas
"A Killer Christmas"

Rookie K-9 Unit

Truth and Consequences
Rookie K-9 Unit Christmas
"Holiday High Alert"

Visit the Author Profile page at Harlequin.com for more titles.

AMISH
CHRISTMAS
HIDEAWAY

LENORA WORTH

HARLEQUIN® LOVE INSPIRED® SUSPENSE

Recycling programs for this product may not exist in your area.

. ® LOVE INSPIRED BOOKS

ISBN-13: 978-1-335-23250-2

Amish Christmas Hideaway

Copyright © 2019 by Lenora H. Nazworth

www.Harlequin.com

Printed in U.S.A.

Why do the heathen rage,
and the people imagine a vain thing?
—*Psalm* 2:1

To all of the friends I've made while writing Amish fiction. Thank you to our loyal readers!

ONE

She'd stopped here on a whim. Tired from a lengthy deposition in Philadelphia, Alisha Braxton planned to find a strong cup of coffee. She needed to stay awake to drive the two hours from the city to the small community of Campton Creek in Lancaster County to celebrate Christmas with her grandmother Bettye Willis.

This quaint Christmas market on the outskirts of Philadelphia beckoned her with the promise of something warm to drink and maybe something wonderful to nibble on while she traveled. Too busy to shop for gifts before now, she decided she'd do a quick browse and buy her grandmother something special. And maybe Mrs. Campton, too.

The two elderly women lived together in the carriage house at the Campton estate, now called the Campton Center. Alisha did several hours a week of pro bono work at the center. It was a good chance to visit with her grandmother and help out the community.

But this week she wouldn't be working as much. A whole week with Granny—a gift from her firm. Five days before Christmas. Her boss had insisted and, as much as she loved her career as an associate with the law firm of Henderson and Perry, Alisha needed a break.

She looked forward to spending the upcoming holidays there with her grandmother, who'd been Judy Campton's assistant for years and now her companion since they were both widowed. A week off and then she'd get back to her paying hours at the small law firm near Reading where she'd worked since law school. The firm was a satellite branch connected to the main firm in Philadelphia. Alisha hoped to work at the big firm one day, but for now she was paying her dues and working her way up the firm's ladder.

Taking in the bright lights lining the marketplace that had once been a town square on the outskirts of Philadelphia, Alisha pulled her small blue sedan into what looked like the last available parking place. A couple strolled by together, holding hands and laughing, packages hanging from their arms. The man smiled down at the woman then tugged at her long dark hair.

A surge of longing hit Alisha, causing her to sit there in the dark while the couple kissed by a stark white sports car parked directly across from Alisha. After putting their packages in the tiny trunk, the man helped the woman into her seat and hurried around to get inside.

They looked so happy, so in love.

Would she ever have that? Probably not. She'd sealed away her heart and focused on work. No time for romance or anything that followed. Once, she'd fallen in love. Once. Putting her memories away, Alisha took in her surroundings.

Dusk moved over the sparkling Christmas trees decorating the tiny square, causing the whole scene to shimmer and glisten. People bundled in scarves and jackets strolled along the busy open market, sipping hot drinks as they laughed and took in the lovely holiday displays. Beautiful but so deceptive. She'd seen the underbelly of life too often lately to appreciate the forced facade of a commercial Christmas. And she sure didn't need to sit here longing for something she'd never have.

"When did I become so jaded?" she said out loud before opening her car door. She needed caffeine and maybe something with pumpkin spice.

She lifted one booted foot out onto the asphalt parking lot, the chilly air hitting her in a burst of December wind. Hoping the snowstorm headed this way would hold off, Alisha watched a vehicle approaching at high speed. The black SUV came to a skidding halt behind the white sports car now trying to back out of the parking space across from where Alisha had just pulled in.

Before she could exit her car, a window came down on the SUV. Then the air shattered with the sound of several rapid-fire gunshots, aimed at the sportscar.

Alisha screamed and sank down in her seat. When the shots kept coming, she crouched low and watched in horror as the couple in the sports car scrambled to find protection.

The gunman kept shooting. And they had no way out.

Alisha looked up and saw the gunman's face in the bright lights from the twinkling decorations and the glow of streetlights. His cold, dead gaze stopped and froze on her.

She got a good look at him.

And…he got a good look at her.

Ducking back down, she held her breath. He'd try to kill her, too. She'd seen him. Bracing for a bullet, she heard people screaming, heard footsteps rapidly hitting the pavement as pedestrians tried to scramble away.

Dear Lord, please help these people and protect me. Help me. Alisha's prayers seemed to freeze in her throat as she waited for more gunshots.

Instead, the vehicle's motor revved and then the dark
SUV spun away, tires squealing, the smell of rubber
burning through the air. Only a few seconds had passed
but the scene played over in Alisha's mind in slow mo-
tion as she relived the sight of that face and then the
screams from inside the tiny car. And then…a stunning
split second of silence.

She heard people running and screaming. Quickly
pulling out her phone, her hands shaking, she called
911 as she wobbled onto her feet and hurried to the car
that now looked like it had been in a war zone, bullet
holes scattered across it, the heavy vinyl convertible
top split and torn.

"A shooting," she said to the dispatcher. "At the
Christmas market near West Fairmount Park." She
named the street and told the dispatcher what had happened. "I… I witnessed the shooting."

People had gathered around and a security guard
stood staring into the car, his expression full of shock.
"What in the world?"

The dispatcher confirmed the location and told Alisha to stay on the phone.

"Officers on the way," Alisha said to the scared guard
after the dispatcher had told her as much. "Secure the
scene and get these people back."

She stepped away, her stomach roiling at the carnage
in the two-seater car. Blood everywhere and both pas-
sengers slumped over, holding each other, their bodies
riddled with bullet holes. They'd been smiling and happy
seconds before and now they were obviously dead.

The other vehicle was long gone but while she waited
she managed to give a description to the dispatcher.

"Large black SUV." She named the model. "A driver

and one shooter but I couldn't make out the license plate. I didn't see anyone else inside."

But she remembered the shooter's face. A light scruffy beard and stringy long dark hair covered by a thick wool cap. His eyes—black as night and dead. So dead inside.

Alisha stayed on the phone but heard the sound of sirens echoing through the chilly night. Her boots crunched against something as she tried to scan the surrounding area. She looked down and saw the delicate, gold-embossed Christmas ornament that had decorated the now-shattered streetlight hovering over the sports car. A star shape, shimmering white.

The ornament laid broken and crushed underneath her feet.

Hours later, Nathan Craig heard a ringing in his ears that would not go away. "Stop it," he groaned, coming awake to find a weak slant of moonlight filtering through the darkness of his bedroom. He wiped at his sleepy eyes and glared at the dial of his watch.

Eleven o'clock.

Exhausted after an all-night surveillance and a day full of reports to his client, he'd gone to bed early and at his own place for once. Now he'd never get back to sleep.

Then he realized his phone was ringing. Not so unusual. Being a private investigator meant he had a lot of late-night calls from either clients or informants. And sometimes, from the angry subjects of his investigations.

Sitting up, he grabbed the annoying device and growled, "This had better be good."

"Nathan?"

The voice was winded and scared, his name a whisper from a raw throat. But that voice held a familiar tone that hit deep in his gut.

"Alisha?"

"Yes."

Now he was wide awake.

Knowing she'd never call him unless she was in trouble or really mad at him again, he said, "Alisha, what's wrong?"

"I... I think someone's trying to kill me," she said, the tremor in her words destroying him.

He stood and grabbed his jeans, hit his toe on a chair and gritted his teeth. "Where are you? Are they after you right now?"

"I'm almost to Campton Creek. Just a few miles from the turnoff. I know they're following me but I don't see the SUV behind me. He'll be back. I saw his face, Nathan. I witnessed a man shoot and kill two people. And you know what that means."

"Hold on," he said, his mind racing ahead while fear held his heart in a vise. "I can be there in fifteen minutes. You stay on the line with me, okay?"

"Okay."

Then he thought better. "Have you called the police?"

She heaved a deep breath. "I had a police escort following me, watching my back. Two officers."

"Where are they now?"

"Dead, I think. Someone shot out their tires and they crashed on the side of the road. The patrol car exploded. I should have stopped to help."

Nathan closed his eyes and tried to focus. "You didn't stop. Smart move."

"I wanted to stop but... I saw the SUV. I sped up and rounded the big curve near Green Mountain." Heaving a sigh that sounded more like a sob, she said, "I pulled off on a dirt lane but it's a dead-end. I think the SUV went on by but I'm afraid to get back on the road."

Nathan knew that curve. Just enough time to get her out of view of any car following her but also a dangerous place where someone could hide and wait for her.

"Did you call anyone else?"

"I called you," she said through a shuddering sob. "Because this won't end with the local police, Nathan. I witnessed a double homicide that looked like a hit job. Those two officers are probably dead. The FBI will probably be called in and I'll need to testify."

FBI? Now he was tripping over his own feet. "Alisha, I know the road you're on. Find an Amish farm and wake someone up. Stay with them until I get there. Do you hear me?"

She didn't speak.

He held the cell between his ear and shoulder while he grabbed at more clothes and found his weapon and wallet.

"Alisha?"

"I know a shortcut," she said, sounding stronger. "I'll take that route once I hit the turn. I'll try to find a house, I promise. My cell battery is low. I have to go."

"Alisha, tell me what to look for."

"Black Denali SUV. Two men in the vehicle. I have to go."

"Alisha, don't—"

She ended the call.

Nathan stood there in the dark, the images playing in his mind a terrible torment. If anything happened to her…

He'd been through this kind of terror before. He would not go there again.

With that vow in mind, he finished putting on his

clothes and hurried out of the cabin toward his big Chevy truck. His heart pumping adrenaline, he headed toward Green Mountain. Once underway, he called his friend Carson Benton at the sheriff's department. While per Pennsylvania law, the deputy couldn't apprehend the suspects, he could serve in tracking them down and alerting the state police and the FBI if needed. He could also help in transporting them if they were apprehended.

Nathan and Carson went way back, had been friends for years. Carson sometimes helped Nathan in an unofficial capacity with missing person cases.

"This had better be good," Carson said, echoing the same words Nathan had uttered about ten minutes ago.

"I need you to check on a woman driving alone and headed toward the turnoff just past Green Mountain, toward Campton Creek. She thinks someone is following her. Someone dangerous. She witnessed a shooting near Philadelphia and she had a police cruiser following her but the perpetrators ran the patrol car off the road."

"Hello to you, too," his longtime friend said with a grunt. "Got it. Who's the woman?"

"Alisha Braxton," Nathan said, one hand on the wheel as he broke the speed limit. Then he described her vehicle. "I'm on my way."

"I know how you drive, Nathan. You'll beat me there," Carson replied in a tart tone. "I'm on it." Then he asked, "Hey, isn't she the one who—"

"Yeah," Nathan said. Then he ended the call.

Alisha Braxton.

The one who got away.

This had to be bad if she'd called him.

Because Nathan knew he was the one man on earth she'd never want to call for help.

* * *

Why had she called him?

Logic told Alisha her first call should have been to 911. But she'd panicked after she'd seen the patrol car behind her bursting into flames and when she'd grabbed for her phone, Nathan had come to mind. He lived close by when he wasn't traveling. Thankful that she'd caught Nathan at home, Alisha knew he could get to her fast. And he'd act first and ask questions later.

He was the kind of man who took matters into his own hands.

He was also the kind of man who broke all the rules, one of the reasons she'd given up on him long ago.

Now it was the only reason she wanted him by her side.

The one man she didn't want to call was also the one man who could help her escape from a couple of killers.

The irony of her situation made her laugh a tiny hysterical laugh while she slipped her car back onto the main road and kept watch behind her. She'd seen the SUV and now it had disappeared. But she wasn't imagining this. If she turned down Applewood Lane and hooked a left back to the old covered-bridge road, she could throw them off. Then she could take the back roads to Creek Road and then Campton Creek proper. She'd be safe soon. She knew these roads, had traveled them as a child.

Had met Nathan in a park out by the creek when they were both in their late teens.

Nathan, who'd been Amish then.

Nathan, who now had few scruples when it came to bringing justice to this world.

He no longer lived among the Amish but for close to fifteen years, he had made it his life's work to always help and protect the Amish. Because he had to help others seek their loved ones so they wouldn't have to live with the pain he carried in his heart.

His younger sister had gone missing after Nathan and his father had fought about his relationship with Alisha. Hannah had been found dead a few weeks later.

Nathan blamed himself. Alisha lived with that same guilt.

She shouldn't have called him tonight. She had her life in order, had her routines down, worked hard, rarely dated. She'd learned to be her own hero. Because she never wanted to go through that kind of pain again, either.

Nathan could complicate all of that.

He could also save her life.

Alisha checked her mirror again and tried to stay calm. She knew how to take care of herself. She'd given the police her statement, described in detail the vehicle and the man she'd seen, left the officers and detectives her contact information and finally had been given permission to leave.

"Will you be all right, Miss Braxton?" one of the detectives at the gruesome scene had asked her.

"I will be when I get to my grandmother's place," she'd replied, glancing around the empty parking lot. The marketplace had been shut down until the crime techs could scour the scene. By then the authorities had questioned all of the witnesses, but most of them had just heard gunshots and seen the SUV speeding out of the parking lot.

Alisha had been the only eyewitness to the murders.

"We can give you an escort," one of the detectives had suggested.

"That might make me feel better," she'd admitted. "It's about two hours from here."

They arranged for a patrol car with two officers to follow her, staying close. She'd watched their car through her rearview mirror, feeling safe, until she'd heard screeching tires and gunshots.

And watched the patrol car careening off the road and into a rocky incline. It had burst into flames.

Now she prayed for those two officers, but she knew in her heart they were probably dead. If the crash hadn't killed them, the shooter would make sure they were dead.

She would be next.

Hurry, Nathan.

When she saw a car approaching, Alisha gasped and watched as it zoomed close. Dark, big, gaining on her.

Alisha couldn't tell who was behind her, but the driver had a lead foot. Coming up on another curve, she took a quick glance in the rearview mirror. The big vehicle was still gaining on her.

Then she saw the headlights of another vehicle off in the distance, coming from the other direction. Her turnoff was up ahead but the on-coming car could be the SUV retracing the same route. Could she make it before either vehicle caught her? She'd have to speed up and make a hard right turn. Checking again, she gauged the distance and monitored the oncoming car, hoping she'd be past it before she spun to the right. Meantime, she prayed the vehicle behind her would keep moving ahead instead of following her.

The night was dark and cloudy, with a possible snow-storm headed across the state. Out here, where few streetlights existed, the hills and valleys looked ominous and misshapen. The ribbon of road twisted and turned and meandered like a giant gray snake.

The vehicle behind her gained speed. When it came close enough to tap her bumper, Alisha let out a gasp and held tight, bracing for a collision. But the vehicle didn't hit her. The driver stayed close but never made contact.

It was now or never.

Taking a breath, Alisha held onto the wheel and watched for the turnoff. Then with a prayer and another gulp of air, she slowed enough to turn the wheels of her car to the right onto the narrow road. Her car wobbled and fishtailed her heart bumping and jumping while she tried to keep control. If she lost the wheel, she'd go careening down into a deep ditch. Or worse, a rocky embankment.

Her nerves tightly knotted, Alisha managed to regain control of the car and stay on the road. Letting out a breath, she gathered her wits and glanced into the rearview mirror. To her dismay, the car that had been approaching from the other direction was now following her.

They'd found her.

TWO

Nathan hit the steering wheel again, wishing Alisha's phone worked. Her battery must have finally fizzled out. He couldn't reach her. But he'd been tailing her for two miles when he looked up and saw another car coming down a hill toward them.

Then he'd watched in horror when Alisha had made a sharp right turn, his heart stopping while he watched her car careening wildly.

She'd made it off the main road and he was headed to follow her when a big dark SUV coming from the other direction turned onto the same route she'd just taken, cutting Nathan off as it whipped in front of his truck.

"No." Nathan slammed on his brakes to avoid a collision and then hit the gas pedal again. "Where are you, Carson?" The deputy sheriff should have been here by now. Carson would have alerted the town police, too, since he didn't have the authority to make any arrests.

But if those men saw the deputy tailing them, they could have shot at Carson, too.

Lord, please protect my friend.

The silent prayer felt foreign and raw inside Nathan's head. He rarely prayed these days, but he still believed deep down inside. Right now, he needed the Lord to hear him on a lot of accounts.

Alisha needed him. He had to get to her.

He slipped and slid onto the turnoff, noting where Alisha's car had gone, his heart doing that jumpy thing it always did each time he came back to the place he'd once called home.

The place where he'd fallen in love with a beautiful *Englisch* girl who had her own dreams and ambitions. The girl who'd walked away from him because she felt as if she'd only remind him of the worst night of his life.

If he didn't find her, *this* would be the worst night of his life. He might have lost his sweet little sister Hannah, but he would not lose Alisha.

Not this time.

Nathan hurried along the dark, deserted road and noted the two vehicles up ahead. The big SUV hovered near Alisha's sedan. He had his weapon concealed in a shoulder holster and he'd shoot first and ask questions later.

When Alisha's vehicle swerved around a curve, Nathan took off and caught up with the SUV following her. While the sleek vehicle inched closer to her, Nathan did the same with the aggressive SUV.

He knew a certain spot up ahead where if he hit at its back bumper just right, he could force the SUV off the road long enough to allow Alisha to get to safety.

Preparing, Nathan kept his eyes on the two cars up ahead. Then he looked in his rearview mirror and saw another vehicle approaching. A traffic jam on this road late at night? Unbelievable. He hoped Carson had found them.

His cell buzzed. Careful to keep his gaze on the road, he let the call come through his truck's Bluetooth.

"I'm behind you," Carson said. "The locals are out in force since they've heard what happened. There's a BOLO out based on the eyewitness description."

"They're following that witness," Nathan replied, relieved for the backup. "I can't let them get to her."

"I'm trying to catch up with them."

"They have to be the same people who killed someone in front of Alisha earlier."

"Why did she come here?" Carson asked.

"She's afraid and…she must have been coming to see her grandmother. I don't know. She panicked, I think."

She had to have panicked to call him, Nathan reasoned.

"Dangerous situation," Carson replied.

"Be careful," Nathan warned. "They're armed."

"I won't do anything stupid," Carson said. "I'm here to observe and help with transport, if needed."

"Okay. I'll tail them until we meet up."

Carson ended the call and sped around Nathan to alert the town police up on the main road out of town. Nathan watched the road ahead. His friend had the authority to stop them for speeding if nothing else. But these people were dangerous. Carson shouldn't take that risk. Smarter to get the police out here.

Nathan focused on the vehicle behind Alisha. The big vehicle bumped against Alisha's car. The driver tried to force her off the road. Nathan gunned his truck, thinking he'd smash into the other vehicle.

Too late.

He watched in horror as the SUV bumped hard against Alisha's sedan again. Unable to help, Nathan shouted as her tiny car went spiraling across the road and headed into a deep ditch.

"No," Nathan said, slamming on the brakes as he came up on the scene.

The SUV took off, speeding away. The town police should be waiting up ahead. Nathan had to check on Alisha.

Nathan put the still moving truck into Park, left it running, and hopped out and hurried toward Alisha, pulling open the driver's-side door.

Nearly out of breath, he called, "Alisha?"

"I'm okay," she said, her hands tight on the steering wheel, her head slumped over. "I'm all right, Nathan."

She didn't sound all right. More like out of breath and going into shock. "I'm calling for help."

"No." Grabbing his arm, she said, "Just get me out of here, please."

He looked at her and then looked down into a dark abyss. She'd somehow managed to stop the car against a jutting rock, but most of the car sat nestled against an old jagged tree trunk. A rotting and weathered trunk that could give at any minute.

Mere inches away from what looked like a sizable drop-off into a ravine.

"I've got you," he said. "C'mon, take my hand."

She nodded. "My bag."

"Okay, grab it. But careful."

She lifted the big businesslike leather bag and handed it to him. Nathan set the bag on the ground and gently tugged at her. "Turn slowly toward me, okay."

She nodded, the car rocking with each movement. Once she twisted and managed to put her legs on the ground, the car moaned and slipped another inch into the old tree trunk.

Nathan's heart slipped right along with the vehicle,

his breath caught. That old stump wouldn't last much longer. "On three," he said. "One, two, three."

His hands on her waist now, he tugged her up and out and then pulled her away from the now shaking car. With a groan and the hissing of tires and metal, the car plummeted against the weak tree trunk, causing the weathered wood to crumble into a hundred powder-dry pieces. Nathan held Alisha down, the sound of the car's front right fender scraping against the rock as it slid over the edge of the ravine and crashed down below with a last moan. A hard crash and then the sound of metal breaking apart echoed out over the hills.

They fell together onto the grass near the curve in the road. Nathan held her close, shut his eyes and took in the sweet scent of her hair.

"Alisha."

She suddenly sat straight up and scooted away from him. "What?"

He lay there, checking her over, the urge to hold her close still strong. "Are you all right?"

"Yes. But my car... It's gone."

Nathan took in her dark golden hair all scattered and wispy around her heart-shaped face. "I'm sorry about that, but I had to get you out. Too late for your car but I need to get you away from here."

Brushing at her hair and clothes, she let out a long, shuddering sigh. "I still owe on that car."

Still practical, he thought, his pulse pounding like a jackhammer in his ear. "You have insurance?"

She gave him a nod, her expression blank now. "Did you call reinforcements?"

"Yes—a friend nearby and the locals waiting down the road. Tell me if you hurt anywhere. Did you hit your head?"

"No. I mean I bumped against something but I'm okay. When they rammed me, I tried to steer the car toward a tree. I found a rock and a tree. Bounced a bit. I could have died if you hadn't come along."

She was shaken but Nathan knew this woman. Tough and stubborn.

"Okay, but you did not die." He stood and offered her his hand. She hesitated and then grabbed on while he tugged her up, the touch of her skin against his fingers jarring him with a current of awareness. "I called my friend Carson Benton. He's a deputy sheriff who helps me out a lot."

"Unofficially, I'm sure. I hope he chased them away."

"Unofficially, yes. I hope they don't shoot him."

Looking her over, he took in the boots and straight black skirt, the tan leather jacket and black turtleneck sweater. Classy. "Alisha, listen, they don't know you're still alive. That gives us time. We need to get you somewhere safe, okay?"

"I'm going to Campton House."

Just as he'd thought, and the closest place to hide for now. "Good. Mrs. Campton has a state-of-the-art security system."

"I know. I told her to get a system installed because of the sensitive nature of some of our cases. It serves as a safe house at times, too."

"Well, that will come in handy since we have to hide you until I can figure this thing out. The longer they think you died in that car, the better our odds of keeping you alive."

"You mean, until *we* can figure this thing out. I'm the one who witnessed a double murder."

He liked her spirit but heard that stubborn tone in her

voice. "And I'm the one who'll protect you and help you find justice. You have to stay hidden."

He took her by the arm. "I'll report the crash from the truck. And before you start up, it's too cold out here to argue about this right now."

"I'm not going to argue," she said. "I'm exhausted."

Nathan's heart went out to her. "Alisha…"

"Don't," she said, holding up a hand. "Don't baby me, Nathan. Just get me to my grandmother's house."

Nathan grunted and let her open her own door. Then he grabbed her big leather bag and hopped in on the driver's side. "Here's your purse."

"This is *not* a purse. It's full of work, my laptop and a flash drive, clothes. And my phone. My life is in this bag."

And hidden chocolate, if memory served him.

"That's a lot of life crammed into one fancy lady purse."

"I don't have a life," she said. Then her gaze met his in sheepish surprise. "It's a briefcase."

"You didn't mean to admit that, did you? The part about not having a life."

"I'm tired. Not making much sense."

"Well, if I have it my way, you'll have a lot of life left in you."

His cell buzzed. "It's Carson." Hitting Accept, he said, "Did you find them?"

Carson's voice came over the Bluetooth connection. "Saw them, followed while the locals gave chase and we had them surrounded."

"But?" Nathan glanced over at Alisha since she could hear the call. Her expression held dread.

"They crashed the SUV near the main highway down the mountain. Got out and ran away on foot. We've got men searching the area and we've called in the K9 unit, but I have a feeling they had another ride coming. It's still not safe." Then he added, "One of the escort officers is alive but critical. The other one died at the scene. I'm sorry, Nathan. The police are up to speed and they've alerted the proper authorities in Philadelphia, including the FBI."

Alisha let out a sob, her hand going to her face.

"Thanks." Nathan said, glancing at Alisha. "I have Miss Braxton with me. I got her out of the car, but it went into the ravine. They'll send someone to circle back around to make sure she's dead. I'd like them to think that for a while. Just until I get her somewhere safe."

"Understood," his friend said. "But you know how this will end, right?"

"Yeah. With me bringing these people to justice." Nathan ended the call and turned to Alisha. "So you heard. Your pursuers managed to escape. You're not safe."

He saw the shudder she tried to hide. "What they did was horrible. I can't get it out of my head." Looking out into the darkness, she whispered, "I should have done something for those officers."

"You did the only thing you could do—you got away. It was probably too late for the one who died at the scene and hopefully, the other one won't die."

He didn't want her to meet that same fate.

"That will be in the news, too. His poor family. To lose him at Christmas. Maybe I should have gone back to Reading."

"No." Nathan couldn't tell her that he was glad to see her, glad to help her. "No. You need to be with family right now."

She nodded, her head down.

"Tell me what you saw tonight," he said in a gentler

tone, wishing he could touch her, hold her and make her feel better.

But that would be the worst idea he'd ever had and he'd had a few bad ones at times.

She nodded and started speaking, her voice strained and weary. Once she'd finished, Nathan couldn't stop himself. He reached over and took her hand. This reeked of a professional hit. But he wouldn't tell her that until he did some digging.

"You'll be safe at the Campton Center for now."

She stared down at his hand and then pulled hers away. "Of course I will. It's solid."

"And I'll be there to make sure."

"What exactly does that mean?"

"That means we'll be spending Christmas together," he replied with a soft smile. "Because I'll be staying there with you until we find these killers."

THREE

"Oh, no," Alisha replied, the shock of his statement overtaking the shock pumping through her body. "That is not going to happen."

"It's happening," he retorted as he took all the back roads she'd planned on taking. "I'm not leaving you alone."

"I won't be alone. I have my grandmother and Mrs. Campton."

"Right. Two elderly ladies who have to use an elevator to get downstairs."

He had a point but Alisha wasn't ready to concede. "And a good security system."

"That helps but we both know a good criminal can work around that."

Right again. But Alisha wasn't about to let him hang around. Yes, she'd called him in a moment of panic but reason was taking over now. "Nathan, I'm a big girl. I can hide out there while I do some checking. For all we know, they might give up on me and go into hiding."

"I'm not willing to wait and see if that happens. Are you?"

She shook her head. "No. I have a week before I go back to the office in Reading the day after Christmas."

"Call your boss and make that two weeks. Just until the New Year."

"I can't do that."

"Yes, you can. Explain the situation. Take some vacation time."

"I'll take the time I have allotted and I'll use that time to track these killers."

"You do realize Christmas is not the time to work, right?"

"Yes. But watching a gunman shoot up a Christmas market five days before the holidays kind of puts a damper on things."

"Are you going to tell the ladies the truth?"

"I have to," she said, hating the idea. "They need to be warned so they can be aware."

"And they need protection, too."

"Maybe I should stay somewhere else."

"No, this is the best plan for now. But, Alisha, I'm going to stay there with all of you whether you like it or not. I know the place has a couple of extra bedrooms in the main house. I'll bunk in one of those."

Bad idea. So why did she feel safer, just knowing he'd be nearby?

Because she was frightened, shaken and… She'd need his help. Nathan Craig was good at his job and he could go where others didn't dare go. He found people. Good people. Scared people. Lost people. And sometimes, the worst of people.

"I can see those wheels turning inside your head," he said when she didn't retort right away. "What are you thinking?"

She twisted to stare at him as they turned onto Creek Road. "I don't have much of a choice. I need you—I mean I need your experience and expertise."

Her head told her to be logical, while her heart shouted that she did need him, too. She'd always needed him.

But she'd been fighting that need since she'd first met him the summer after her senior year. Funny, how he'd been on the fringes of her life for most of her life. Around but always out of her reach. Once, they'd been so close. Teenage sweethearts. But they were both adults now. Professional and on a case. Nothing more. Because neither one of them had anything more to give.

Tonight, he'd saved her. Alisha couldn't forget that.

"Don't worry," he said in a tight tone, as if he knew exactly what she was thinking. "I'll stay out of your way. I'll have plenty to keep me busy."

Justice. The man always wanted justice.

Well, so did she, but she sure hadn't planned on getting it with Nathan's help. She didn't want to spend her holidays chasing after a killer, but her instincts told her the murderers would keep chasing after her.

"I'll be busy, too," she said. "I just want this over."

"Are you referring to this murder investigation or being forced to keep me around?"

"Both," she admitted.

Nathan pulled the truck up to the quiet, looming house and switched off the motor. "We'll have to wake them and I'll need to hide my truck in the garage."

Alisha stared at the stately redbrick mansion trimmed in white columns, the rows of tall windows now looking vulnerable instead of comforting, the big evergreen wreath on the door reminding her of all the holidays she'd spent here.

Too many memories for tonight, coupled with Nathan being here beside her. A great weight of fatigue and shock pushed at her soul. "Yes. Let's get inside and do what we have to do."

Nathan quickly came around the truck and opened her door, his gaze scanning the old oaks and high shrubs and then the driveway and parking areas. "At least the backyard is gated and fenced."

"We have security lights and alarms everywhere."

He helped her down, his hands on her waist. Alisha stared up and into his eyes, really seeing him for the first time in a long time. He had always been good-looking, but that world-weary cragginess that shadowed his face made him handsome and mysterious. His eyes, so cobalt blue and shimmering, held too many secrets and his dark hair, always unruly, curled against his neck. A rogue sweep of heavy bangs shielded his frown while his gaze held hers.

He was off-limits and yet, right now, she wanted to reach up and brush those thick curls off his forehead.

"Thank you, Nathan," she said instead.

"You can thank me when this is all over," he replied, removing his hands as if he'd been burned.

Alisha accepted that, the loss of his touch already moving through her with aching clarity. Grabbing her briefcase, she hurried to the double doors of the carriage house entryway, where an open portico separated the garage and the upstairs apartment from the main house. Glancing up at the enclosed upper breezeway, which allowed people to move from the garage and second-floor apartment to the main house during bad weather, Alisha breathed deeply and shivered in the late-night cold. She had a key but she rang the bell instead so she wouldn't scare her grandmother by slipping into the house.

"Alisha?"

Hearing her grandmother's sweet voice over the intercom brought tears to Alisha's eyes. "Yes, Granny. It's me. Sorry I'm so late."

"Come on up," Bettye said, buzzing the door open.

Relief filled Alisha's soul but with it came the letdown of adrenaline and the horrible realization of what she'd witnessed. Her hands started shaking but she held her briefcase with a death grip to keep from falling apart.

Nathan stepped up and placed his arm across her shoulder, tugging her close. He then took the heavy bag. "I've got you," he whispered as he pushed open the door for her. "Don't fall apart on me now, okay?"

Alisha swallowed her fears and the delayed reaction to everything she'd been through in the last few hours. "I'll be all right." She didn't want to fall apart and she didn't want him to be kind to her.

But she didn't push him away. She *did* need Nathan. And not just to help her stay alive. The strength of his grip reminded her that he'd once made her feel so secure. That feeling had returned tonight, but she'd have to get it out of her system.

Bettye Willis met them at the landing where the stairs from the portico doors met the second floor in a wide entryway. A small table held a sparkling ceramic Christmas tree, the smell of cinnamon-and-spice potpourri lingering in the air.

Bettye took Alisha into her arms in a tight hug. "Alisha, we were beginning to get worried." Stepping back to get a good look, she said, "I sent Judy on to bed."

Then her grandmother saw Nathan there in the shadows. Her surprised gaze moving from Alisha to him, Bettye asked, "Mr. Craig, what are you doing here?"

Nathan smiled at Bettye. "That's a long story, Mrs. Willis."

"He's here to help me, Granny," Alisha said, hoping her grandmother wouldn't press. "We can explain in the morning."

Bettye scoffed that away. "I was up reading," she said. "Come into the kitchen and I'll make you something to eat. And then you can tell me what's really going on."

When they hesitated, her grandmother put her hands on her hips. "You do realize that while I'm old, I'm not completely hapless and senile. Alisha, you would not bring Nathan Craig here in the middle of the night without an extremely good reason."

Alisha shot Nathan a warning glance. "I'll explain then, Granny. No need to keep you up all night wondering."

"That's unbelievable," Bettye said after Alisha retold what had happened to her. Turning to where Nathan sat in front of a half-eaten roast beef sandwich, she patted his hand. "I'm so thankful Alisha thought to call you, Nathan."

Nathan stared at the cookie waiting by his plate and then glanced at Alisha, concern hitting him in the gut. What if he hadn't answered his phone? What if he hadn't been at the cabin?

He wouldn't think about that. He was here now with her and she was safe. "Me, too, Mrs. Willis."

"Call me Bettye," the older woman said. She wore a blue flannel robe to keep warm in the wee-hour chill of the spacious art deco–style kitchen. "More coffee?"

Nathan held up his cup, thinking he wouldn't get much sleep tonight anyway. "Thank you."

Alisha sat holding her mug, absorbing the warmth. Her grandmother had found her a cozy sweater and a pair of jeans. Alisha kept some clothes here since she often worked pro bono into the late hours and spent the night now and then.

"So, you're going to be our protector," Bettye said, nodding her head. "We'll explain all of this to Mrs. C in the morning. She'll certainly agree that this is the safest place for both of you right now."

"I don't want to put you or her in any danger, Granny," Alisha said. "This is just for a couple of days."

"Until after Christmas," Bettye said. "Remember, you have the whole week off."

"Maybe until the New Year," Nathan repeated again.

"I hope it won't take that long," Alisha replied, a stubborn glint in her green eyes.

"No matter," her feisty grandmother replied. "As you know, Alisha, the center will be closed for the next few days and we have lots of baking to do and packages to wrap. We go visiting the Amish during Christmas. You can help with all of that."

"Okay, Granny," Alisha said. But her voice held little enthusiasm. She would work day and night to solve this thing.

"I'll take a room in the main house," Nathan said to Bettye. "But at least I'll be on the premises."

"I feel better already," Bettye replied. "Now, let's get you both settled in. I'm sure you are exhausted. We'll continue this discussion in the morning." Getting up, she added, "You two must not have been hungry."

"I'll save my cookie for later," Nathan said.

"I'm sorry, Granny. Hard to eat." Alisha took her own sandwich to the sink. "I'll do the dishes and then I'm going to my room."

Nathan lifted his eyebrows, questioning.

"Relax," Alisha said. "My room is right across from Granny's. This place has three bedrooms. The big suite where Mrs. Campton stays and two smaller bedrooms across the hallway, with a bath and small sitting room between them."

"It's quite cozy," Bettye said with a shrug.

"Yeah, cozy. I vaguely remember the layout." Nathan thought of all the things that could go wrong. "Do I need a key or a code to get to the main house?"

"I'll show you," Alisha said, her tone anxious.

"I'll wait here then," Bettye said, her grandmotherly gaze taking in all the undercurrents flowing around them. "Then we'll lock up tight."

Nathan nodded and thanked Bettye for the food. "I'll be close if you need anything."

Remembering the house from his time here before, Nathan guided Alisha to the glass door that led to the enclosed breezeway, where two rows of windows provided views of the big front yard and the sprawling tree-lined backyard and lighted pool area.

"Too many windows," he said, holding her elbow while he scanned their surroundings.

"I've never worried about that before," Alisha admitted. "Granny will feel better, having you close by."

They made it to the matching set of doors on the other side of the breezeway, bypassing wicker chairs and tall parlor ferns.

Alisha keyed in the code and the doors clicked open. Then they moved into the upper hallway of the estate house, now a center to help the Amish and anyone else who didn't have the money to pay for doctors, lawyers and counselors.

"The elevator is to the left if you ever need it," Alisha reminded him, her words echoing over the big upstairs floor. Then she pointed to the right. "There are two bedrooms on the front of the house. And two more on the back. The master is up here on the other side down another hallway. It faces the backyard. We put mothers with children in there."

"I'll take one to the front," he said, "since the back should be fairly secure, but the front yard could be compromised."

Alisha nodded and took him to a bedroom that had a direct view to the street and to the carriage house. The yard was well lit, at least.

"Sheets and towels are in the linen closet in the bathroom," she said, pointing to the adjoining door. Then she turned at the main door. "I guess I'll see you in the morning."

Nathan reached for her arm. "Are you sure you're all right?"

Alisha nodded but he could see the fatigue and worry shadowing her eyes. "I'm good now that I'm here. I doubt I'll sleep but I'll be okay."

"I can walk you back across," he offered.

"You don't need to do that."

"I'll go as far as the doors to the breezeway, to be sure."

She nodded and they walked back up the hallway together.

"This is an amazing house," he said once they'd reached the breezeway.

Alisha nodded. "The Camptons founded this town over a century ago. It's sad to think the Admiral and Mrs. Campton lost their only son Edward. He was killed in Afghanistan. He was a navy SEAL."

"I've heard about him," Nathan replied. "I still have friends around here who tell me the latest news."

"And family?"

Her question threw Nathan. They never discussed the past.

"A few," he said. "My parents will always be here."

He was about to tell her good-night when he heard a noise outside and then saw a flash of light.

Without thinking, he pushed Alisha down beneath the windows and went with her, shielding her.

"Someone is in the front yard," he whispered, his heart hammering. "Don't move."

Alisha nodded. "Granny—"

Nathan put a finger to her lips, his grip on her so tight he felt her heart beating against his. "I'm going to check it out. You stay right here."

Alisha gave him a wide-eyed frown. "Nathan, don't do that."

When they heard another noise, he gave her a quick nod.

"If I'm not back in five minutes, call 911, okay?"

Then he turned and headed back across the breezeway so he could sneak out the garage door downstairs, the beat of Alisha's heart still racing through his pulse.

If these goons had found her here this quickly, how did he have any chance of protecting her and keeping her alive?

FOUR

Alisha huddled underneath the windows, the cold floor making her shiver while fear for Nathan made her shudder. Should she go after him? Alert her grandmother? Find a weapon?

Granny. What if someone hurt her grandmother?

Deciding a weapon would be good, just in case, she hurried back into the big, dark house and went to the master bedroom. Moving past the eerie glow of all the sconces, she stood at the bedroom door and spotted the big fireplace inside. Then she hurried to find the fire poker.

The wieldy iron poker in her hands, she slipped to the windows lining the room and checked the sloping backyard. Shadows cascaded out over the grass and shrubs to reveal a quiet stillness. The yellow glow of the security lamps gave her courage. But she needed to get back to the front of the house and check on her grandmother and Nathan. Had it been five minutes?

Alisha moved quickly back up the wide hallway, going past the stairs. When she heard a noise coming from the front yard, she stopped. Should she go down or call 911?

Before she could decide, a strong arm pulled her

close. She tried to scream but the sound caught in her throat. Then a hand clamped down over her mouth and a man breathed close.

Frantic, she tried to raise the poker.

"Be still and don't make a sound."

Nathan.

He released her and touched his finger to her lips. Then he whispered close. "I've got this."

Relieved but wanting to kick him for scaring her, Alisha whispered, "Who was out there?"

"Carson," he said. "He was done with the search and decided to drive by to see if we'd made it here safely. But he did spot a prowler. We met up in the front yard. He's still out there rattling around."

"Why didn't you just say that instead of scaring me?"

"I didn't want to startle you and cause you to scream."

"What makes you think I'd scream?"

"Why didn't you stay put?"

Tired and still shaking, she glowered at him. "I went to get this," she said, holding up the poker. Her hand shook so she held it down again.

Nathan's frown darkened. "I told you to stay where you were."

"I was worried about you and my grandmother. I had to do something." Then she checked him over. "What happened?"

"I'm fine. The prowler ran away and got in a vehicle about a block from here. Carson's off-duty, working on his own time to see if he can find any prints."

He took the poker from her. "Are you all right?"

Nodding, she turned toward the breezeway. "I need to check on Granny."

"I went over there when I couldn't find you," he said.

"Her door is closed. The lower door is still locked. Everything's okay over there."

Nathan's phone buzzed. "Carson, all clear inside. I'll meet you at the front door."

Alisha followed Nathan down the stairs and put in the code to unlock the door.

The deputy came in, shivering and nodding. "So we had a visitor."

"Yep." Nathan turned to Alisha. "Alisha, this is my friend Deputy Carson Benton."

Alisha shook the man's hand, noticing he was about the same age as Nathan but his hair was clipped and close-cut and he was built like a linebacker. "Thank you for all of your help, Deputy Benton."

"Call me Carson," the deputy said with a smile. "Nasty business, but we'll get things going. The town police will want to get your statement, Miss Braxton. We can do that in the morning." Then he glanced toward Nathan. "And we can talk more in the morning. I want to help but I'll need information."

"Why not now?" Alisha said. "I can't sleep and it's quiet here. We can go in the office."

Carson's stern expression never changed but his gaze moved to Nathan. Did he have to get the PI's approval? "I'll need to call the officers who worked the scene where your car went over. They'll be the ones working this side of the case."

"I would expect all of you to follow proper protocol," Alisha replied, daring Nathan to argue with her.

"You heard the woman," Nathan said. Then he turned to Alisha. "I know you're antsy but you're gonna crash and burn if you don't get some rest."

"I want to find these killers," she replied, moving ahead of them. But she couldn't deny that she was sink-ing fast. Turning at the stairs leading down, she waited. "The sooner I get this report done, the sooner I *can* rest."

Carson shook his head and shrugged at Nathan. "We all agree on that." He walked aside to call in one of the officer who'd been on the scene earlier.

Alisha motioned them along the downstairs central hall. Soon they were settled in the big office that used to belong to Admiral Campton. She kept the blinds closed and turned on a desk lamp while she wondered if someone could still be lurking around out there.

Once the other officer arrived, they all sat down across from the desk, quiet and observant until they got down to business.

Officer Cantor looked sleepy, his salt-and-pepper hair thick and unruly. "Once I take your statement, I can work with the state police to get on with this investigation. They'll put out an APB on the vehicle Nathan described, the same one you saw. The Philly police issued a BOLO on the two suspects who are now wanted for the double homicide that you witnessed and for murdering a police officer and injuring another one, and for your attempted murder. We've got men searching the woods but I have to believe whoever showed up here tonight had to have been one of those men. Or both."

"They might not even realize we came here since my truck is hidden in the garage," Nathan said. "Maybe they were looking to steal a ride."

"Or finish the job," Carson pointed out.

"So let's start at the beginning," Officer Cantor said. "I know you told the LEOs back in Philadelphia what happened but whatever information you can give the town police will help them to coordinate with Philly to make sure we're after the same driver and shooter, got it?"

Alisha nodded. "I'm a lawyer. I've got it."

Carson's appreciative glance eased her worries a little. She had to wonder what Nathan had told his friend about her. She wondered about a lot of things regarding Nathan Craig. He was back in her world in a big way so she needed to handle this with a logical approach. Not a good time to get all tangled up in the past and what might have been.

For the next few minutes, she talked about what had happened hours ago in Philadelphia. When she was finished, she had no energy left. Retelling the horror of watching two people die had outdone her.

Nathan held up his hand. "That's enough for now. Alisha needs to get some rest. I'll stand guard."

"You need to sleep, too," she said, glad he was here but still holding out reservations on how this was going to work.

"I don't sleep much," he said, his tone quiet, his eyes shuttered.

"Okay." His friend stood and crossed his arms over his chest while Officer Cantor gathered his things. "You two work out the details on who's more tired and I'll get back with you tomorrow to see how you're doing."

Alisha didn't argue. "Thank you, Deputy Benton and Officer Cantor." Then she added, "You'll probably hear from the Philadelphia FBI field office. I'm more than willing to talk to them, too."

"We can arrange that," Officer Cantor said. "Bring you into the station."

Nathan walked them to the side door and then came back to where she stood in the hallway. "Okay, upstairs. You need sleep."

Alisha wanted to fuss at him but fatigue made her

dismiss that idea. She had a feeling they'd have lots of discussions before this was over.

When would it be over?

Nathan walked her back to the upstairs door to the carriage house. "Alisha."

"I'm all right, Nathan. I just want a shower and sleep."

"Okay." He turned to go across the breezeway, but pivoted to stare outside, checking. "It's snowing," he said.

Alisha looked through the windows on both sides of the wide room. "So it is. I used to stand here on nights like this, waiting for the snow to fall. This has always been a beautiful place, the one place where I felt loved and happy."

"Alisha," he said again, something raw in the way he said her name. "I know you don't want me here but... I can't leave now. This is dangerous, too dangerous. You have to know that we might not be able to stay here."

"*I* might not be able to stay here," she retorted, her heart battling a mighty war. "You can go on about your business."

"No, I can't," he said, his tone sharp. "I'm in it now. They know my vehicle and they must know I brought you here."

What if they hurt Nathan? She hadn't considered that he was in trouble, too. "I shouldn't have involved you. I wasn't thinking straight."

"I don't mind being involved and I want to find these people, same as you. We have to work together and that means we might have to leave together."

So he could protect her and seek justice, not because he wanted to be near her. She wished she'd never called him. "But we don't know who was out there in the yard."

"Yes, we do. They sent someone here because they

know everything about you now. The minute you looked into that hit man's eyes, they started digging and now you're on their list."

"So you believe this was a professional hit?" She'd suspected that herself.

He lifted his chin. "The way you described it, the way they came after you, yes. It had to be."

Alisha leaned against the door jamb. "This is bad. I should have left and gone far away from here."

"But you didn't. I'm glad you didn't. Now I can help you and protect you… That is, if you let me."

With that he turned and went to the other side of the rambling old house.

Alisha shivered and closed the door between them, thinking there was a lot more between them than just a hallway in a house.

More like a lifetime of regret and longing across a broken bridge that couldn't be mended.

God, if you had to send me a hero, thank you for sending this one. Even if I didn't want him here. Thank You, Lord.

With that prayer centered in her head, she went into the tiny room with the window alcove she'd always loved, showered, threw on some old pajamas then sprawled across the purple chenille spread her grandmother had turned down.

And promptly fell into a troubled, nightmarish sleep.

Nathan sat in a chair by the window in the room across the house from Alisha, his eyes burning from fatigue while he noticed every little thing in the muted darkness below. The snow silenced most of the noises, but years of stakeouts and doing surveillance that kept him up in the wee hours made him tense and alert. He'd told Alisha the truth. He never slept well.

While he sat in the shadows, he remembered the girl he'd fallen in love with. He'd been willing to give up his way of life for this girl but as it turned out, he'd had to give up the Amish community for another reason. That reason had opened a chasm between Alisha and him, all of their dreams shattered and broken in one long horrible night.

A night so different from this one but full of the same kind of fear and angst.

Summer. With a full moon and the world at his feet.

Sitting there, he drifted into sleep, his memories an aching reminder of the family he'd left behind. Just a few miles from here but so far away.

He thought of Alisha with her long golden-brown hair and bright green eyes, laughing in the wind, her sundress long and flowing. He'd been out in the garden right here helping his father work the soil and plant a butterfly garden for Mrs. Campton. Alisha had been visiting her grandmother and she'd been sitting by the pool, reading a book but also watching them at work.

He'd met her briefly once before when her grandmother had come calling at his family's house. And he'd never forgotten looking into her pretty eyes.

Now she was staring at him, smiling at him.

After he'd clumsily dropped a whole crate of plants and sent dirt flying everywhere, she'd hopped up to help him salvage what he could before his father saw what had happened. They'd become fast friends and Nathan had gone home with a big crush on a girl he was forbidden to like.

"You're different, Nathan. You're like no one I've ever met."

He'd felt the same about her. Always.

We were so young and carefree that summer.

And so naive.

Nathan came awake with a start. Had he heard something outside? Or had he been dreaming?

Standing, he grunted in pain, every muscle in his body protesting. Wiping at his eyes, he noticed the time on his watch. Four in the morning. He'd slept in this cushioned chair for over an hour.

Wide awake now, he studied the front yard and saw that it was now covered in snow. No alarms had sounded and the motion-detection lights hadn't triggered.

He was imagining things.

But his gut told him to be cautious so he washed his face and decided he'd do a walk through the old house and wait for the sun to come up.

For good measure, he grabbed his weapon. He'd been licensed to carry a concealed weapon for years now but he rarely had to use the thing. Still, he'd learned that being out alone in the wee hours could be dangerous.

He padded in his socks up the wide upstairs hallway, the wooden floors creaking here and there underneath his weight.

He made it to the master bedroom and took his time checking on the backyard. It stretched like a white blanket down to the deep creek that ran through this town. He remembered swimming and fishing in that creek with his younger siblings.

"Tag, you're it."

"I'll find you," Nathan would call to his two younger brothers. He'd always been the one who looked after the *kinder*.

Then he thought of Hannah.

"Nathan, do not leave us. We love you. You must

not leave. What about me, Nathan? I won't have my big brother. Don't go. Please don't go."

Tears formed in his eyes. He'd left his little sister crying. "I'll find you, Nathan. I'm come and bring you home."

Only she'd become the one who'd never returned.

Too many thoughts crowding his mind. He'd never planned to be back here under these circumstances.

Nathan turned back and went downstairs, amazed at the size of this mansion. He checked two other bedrooms and then moved toward the large den where a massive fireplace took center stage. Beyond the den with all of the family portraits and fancy trinkets and treasures, he saw the sunroom that formed a rectangle at the back of the house.

More windows here, rows and rows of them, with two sets of French doors leading out to the terrace and a huge pool that was covered for winter.

The yard looked the same from the lower floor, white and stark against the security lights. But he knew a criminal could be hiding out there, alarms or no alarms.

He headed to the front of the house and went to the dining room window to peek through the heavy curtains.

Then he saw something that had him on high alert again.

A fresh set of heavy footprints had marred the beauty of the new-fallen snow. Someone has passed through the front yard while he'd been moving through the house.

FIVE

Nathan hurried upstairs and across the breezeway, checking both sides of the yard as he went. Nothing in the back and nothing, no one, in the front. Maybe someone walking to work had cut through the yard, but this place was so stately and secluded he doubted that. The Amish would respect the property and stay on the roads or sidewalks. Anyone else would drive to work. Why would anyone walk through the snow on private property this early in the morning?

Knocking softly on the door, he waited, hoping Alisha would hear and check through the peephole since her room was the closest. When he heard movement behind the door, he did another sweep of the front yard. Other than those glaring, man-size footprints in the powdery white, the world looked serene and safe. Like a Christmas card.

Alisha opened the door, a cup of coffee steaming in her hand, her expression wary. "What are you doing?"

"I couldn't sleep." He swept past her. "What are *you* doing up?"

"I couldn't sleep much, either. I've been up a while."

Not into small talk, he said, "I saw footprints down in the snow."

She puttered in thick red socks to the windows of the tiny sitting room across from the big kitchen.

Nathan tugged her back. "Hey, don't get too close to the windows."

"I want to see."

"Trust me—the footprints go right through the yard."

Giving him a sleepy stare, she said, "What should we do?"

"Nothing for now since they're gone and we don't know if they were just passing through or not." He eyed the coffee.

"Go get a cup," she said, reading his mind.

Soon, they were nestled in the dainty sitting room. The deep burgundy brocade covering the furniture looked old and comfortable, worn in all the right places but adorned with feminine things like doilies and crocheted blankets. He watched as Alisha curled up with one of the blankets, papers and folders scattered all around her.

Nathan inhaled a sip of the good coffee and then watched her while the brew burned all the way to his stomach. "What have you been working on?"

She gathered the papers and shoved them to the side. "A case regarding a divorce. Nothing for you to worry about."

"And this?" He pointed to a bullet-point list and skimmed the information. "You're building a case for what happened last night, right?"

"I'm jotting down things as I remember so I can sort through them, yes."

"That's very lawyerly of you."

She took a long sip of her coffee. "Did you sleep at all, Nathan?"

"No, but the one time I did fall asleep someone de-

cided to take an early morning stroll through the yard.
Some bodyguard I am."

"You don't have to do this. I don't expect you to watch
me 24/7."

For a brief instant, he wondered what it would be like
to have her around day and night. But he pushed that
dream away, like he always did at three in the morning
when he ached with loneliness and hopelessness. "I told
you already, I want to do this."

Picking up her list, she studied it for a moment and
then dropped it back on the couch. "I stopped there to
get coffee last night. I wanted to shop since I'd been so
busy. Everything looked so pretty. Like Christmas. I
thought it would put me in the spirit."

Nathan's heart, so hardened and withered, crumbled a
bit. She wasn't ready or willing to collapse and she sure
wouldn't do it with him in the room. She'd always been
strong, sure, secure. Now her world had been shattered.

Now he was back in her world and she would fight
him every step of the way. "You can talk to me, you
know."

She bobbed her head in acceptance. "I don't even
know the names of the victims. I mean, I heard the crime
scene people talking, but I don't remember. I remember
so many details, so why can't I recall that? I need to find
out who those people were."

"We can do that," Nathan said, thinking the shock
was still messing with her head. "We'll get a full report
and compare what you told the police to what the police in Philadelphia have. You can stay in contact with
all of them, but you don't have to leave here to do that."

"We won't get anything done if we don't go into action."

"I say we lie low here today," he told her. "You need

some time with your grandmother. I'll start digging into things."

"I want to dig with you."

"Well, we can do that but first, try to relax and enjoy being here, okay?"

"Is that possible after last night?"

"I said *try*."

"I won't put them in danger."

"I'm going to map out a way for us to slip out of here if we need to do so. I'll also coordinate with the police about beefing up security for them if we do run."

"I don't plan to spend the rest of my life on the run," she said. Standing, she held her cup and watched the dawn breaking, careful to stay back from the opening in the drapery. "It looks so peaceful out there, doesn't it?"

"Yes."

"But that's the thing about life. The surface covers so much more. So many undercurrents and hidden things. That couple last night obviously had it all but they knew something—or were hiding something—that caused someone else to want to murder them."

"Or they could have done things that made someone extremely angry."

Nathan also wondered if the couple had witnessed events they didn't need to see or if they'd managed to make dangerous people put a hit on them. Probably both.

Thinking about Alisha's jaded view of life, he waded through the undercurrents in this room. His chest hurt with trying to breathe while being this close to Alisha again. As grim as it was, working on this murder would help him to clear his head. He'd barely had time to process being in her life again or having her back in his in such a shocking way. The last time he'd seen her here, they'd both wound up working on a missing person case involving an abandoned baby in the Amish community up the road. He'd found the young mother and reunited her with her older brother, who was now married and raising the girl's baby with his new wife.

He and Alisha had worked together, grudgingly. But they both wanted the same things—justice and helping those in need.

"Are you hungry?" Alisha asked, her gaze touching on his face and moving on.

"Starving."

"I can cook some eggs and toast. Maybe some bacon."

"I'd like that."

They moved to the kitchen and worked in a comfortable silence since Alisha didn't want to wake her grandmother or Miss Judy. But the smell of coffee and bacon acted like an alarm clock.

"Well, what do we have here?"

Nathan turned to find Alisha's grandmother smiling at them, hope in her crystal blue eyes. She wore the same robe that covered her from neck to feet and fuzzy reindeer slippers complete with red noses.

"Granny," Alisha said, smiling for the first time since Nathan had entered the apartment. "Did we wake you?"

"Child, I have been getting up at five-thirty in the morning for most of my life," Bettye said as she shuffled into the kitchen and found a mug. It read: Be Still and Know. The mug had a butterfly motif on it. "But I have to admit, that bacon smells good."

Nathan smiled and flipped the bacon onto a plate lined with paper towels. Used to eating solitary meals, he enjoyed the coziness of this kitchen. Too much.

Bettye filled her cup and glanced down the long hallway. "I usually wake Judy around six-thirty. She has a nurse who comes and helps her with her bath and makes

sure she's had her medication. She still insists on dressing for the day—usually in a pastel pantsuit. I fix her
a tray for breakfast and make a light lunch, sit with her
while I knit or crochet and then I cook supper. We watch
television—she loves romantic movies—and I read to
her in her room. We lead a pretty boring life."

"Sounds good to me," Nathan said while he delivered
the bacon with a flourish to the small four-top breakfast
table. "Your food is ready, madame."

Bettye giggled like a schoolgirl and came to sit by
him. "It's so good to see you again, Nathan. I know we
run into each other from time to time, but having you
here is a blessing despite the reason for you being here."

Nathan knew Bettye Willis to be a good, faithful
woman even though she'd done the same as him—
jumped the fence and left the Amish. He appreciated
her sweet declaration. She'd found love and happiness in
the outside world but she'd sacrificed seeing her Amish
family since she'd moved here from another community. Her husband Herbert had been alive when Nathan
first met Alisha. A great man with a larger-than-life per-
sonality. He had worked for the Camptons, too, as their
maintenance man and groundskeeper.

"I'm glad to be here," Nathan said, glancing at Alisha. "I hope we can find these people before they com-
mit any more crimes."

Bettye buttered her toast. "I'll explain to Judy when I
go in to wake her. She's fuzzy in the mornings but once
she gets going, she is still wise and spry."

Alisha sat down beside her grandmother. "Nathan
and I plan to work in the main office today, Granny. We
want to crack this thing but we have to be watchful."

"Of course you do," Bettye said. "I have plenty of
supplies for the holidays, so I'll cook us a hearty sup-

per. Judy loves company and she's looking forward to seeing you, Sugar-bear."

Alisha's eyes widened in embarrassment as she looked over at Nathan, a becoming blush moving over her face.

Nathan couldn't stop his grin. "You hear that, Sugar-bear? Supper cooked by the best of the best. We're in for a treat."

"If you call me that again, you won't be invited to supper," she retorted, but her eyes held a twinkle.

Bettye smiled her sweet smile and sipped her coffee.

Nathan remembered calling Alisha that long ago after he'd heard her grandfather calling her Sugar-bear.

And Bettye Willis must have remembered, too, since she looked pretty smug and proud of herself. Matchmaking during a murder investigation.

That was a new one.

Alisha silently cringed while she washed up the breakfast dishes. *Sugar-bear?* Why had Granny brought up that old nickname?

Maybe because the handsome man sitting at the breakfast table had made her grandmother's pragmatic mind go completely giddy?

Nathan had that effect on people. Which made him a great investigator since he could get people to talk, but it also made him too dangerous for most women.

She should know. She'd been smitten with him ten years ago and even now, when they were forced to come face to face on cases, she had to fight not to revert back to being a wide-eyed schoolgirl.

Deciding that couldn't happen, she hurriedly got dressed and gathered her files, shoving them into her briefcase. Her grandmother wanted her to find love and be happy but pushing Nathan back at her wouldn't take Alisha back down that road. The man had a quest that took all of his time. And she had her own sense of justice which meant long hours and sleepless nights. She was still an associate at the law firm since she'd only been practicing a couple of years. But one day she hoped to make partner. Which reminded her, she needed to call her boss and explain what was going on here before anyone saw it on the news.

"I'm so glad we got to visit," her grandmother said from the kitchen when Alisha came out of her bedroom. Granny was making cinnamon bread, one of Alisha's favorites. The place smelled divine.

"So am I," Miss Judy said from her dainty chair by the small fireplace. "What a good day to stay in and bake."

Judy sent Alisha a soft smile. Even in old age, Judy Campton as still a regal, beautiful woman. Her hair was white now but clipped in a precise short bob. She wore a blue cashmere sweater and her famous pearls, classic and commanding. "Can you come and sit by me before you head to work, darling?"

"Of course." Alisha crossed the room to settle on the ottoman by the chair. "I hope we didn't upset you with our news, Miss Judy. I won't let anything happen to either of you."

Judy scoffed at that. "Alisha, your grandmother and I are tough old birds. We've seen a lot in our lives. We have faith that God is always in control."

"His will, not ours," Bettye echoed, her hands moving with grace over the bread dough. Granny still had the Amish doctrine ingrained in her.

Judy patted Alisha's hand. "You are safe here. Your grandmother and I will pray all day while you and your handsome protector do what needs to be done. God gave us brains to help in His work, you know. You might be terrified, but He put you in that spot at that time for a reason, Alisha. You fight for the underdogs and you fight for those who can't help themselves. You will bring these evil people to justice."

"I hope so," Alisha said. "It's something I can't get out of my mind. I've worked a lot of cases since law school, but seeing a murder will stay with me a long time."

"Seeing justice done will help you come to terms with that image," Judy said. "Now we have security and Mr. Craig has assured me the authorities are aware of the situation. I can rest easy and enjoy all those cute Christmas movies on television. You know, they are so romantic."

Alisha laughed at that. "I rarely have time to watch but my friends sometimes force me to sit for popcorn and love stories."

"We all have love stories," Judy said, nodding. "You have one yourself."

"I think I'm a little late for the love department," Alisha said, thinking of the man waiting for her on the other side of the house. "I love my work so I'd better get going."

"All work and no romance can make a girl tuckered out," Granny said. "Be kind to Nathan, Sugar-bear. He still cares about you."

Alisha wasn't sure how to answer that, so she said, "I'm thankful that he's here, that's for sure."

"Yes, we are too," Miss Judy said with a serene smile. "Bettye, finish up and we'll watch this movie while the bread rises."

Alisha left them talking back and forth about which holiday movies they loved the most.

She really did need to get a life outside of her brief-case. And she really needed to get a handle on the way Nathan made her heart bump and skip all at the same time.

I'm fighting a battle, Lord. Please give me the strength to stay away from temptation.

But when she got to the office across the way, that temptation was sitting on the old leather loveseat with his eyes closed and his booted feet across an ottoman straight in front of him.

Alisha had to swallow. He looked so at peace, asleep there in the sunlight that had slipped through the blinds. So beautiful, so young, so amazing.

Was he as soul-weary as she felt?

Had God brought them together for a reason besides finding a killer?

Get to work, she told herself. *Focus on what needs to be done. Or you won't live to figure out that question.*

Standing here, watching Nathan sleep, Alisha sure wanted to live for a long time to come.

SIX

Nathan woke with a start and tried to remember where he was. Campton House. He sat up, removed the blue chenille throw someone had placed over him then rubbed his hand down his face.

The office, with midmorning sunshine streaming through the blinds, its brilliance casting off the last of the snow. Everything came back to him and he became fully awake, a panic setting in.

Where was Alisha?

The office door stood open and the house breathed quietly, the few creaks and sighs from old age as comfortable as the air around him. But that sinister shadow of death and fear surrounded him too and he jumped up, hit his boot against the coffee table and mumbled to himself as pain shot through his already sore toe.

Hurrying to the hallway, he called out. "Alisha?"

No answer.

Nathan sprinted up the long hallway toward the kitchen, his breath catching against his chest. Why had he fallen asleep?

"Alisha," he called again.

"In here," she said, emerging from the powder room

midway between the kitchen and the office. "I'm sorry. I was taking a break."

Seeing the concern and surprise in her wide eyes, Nathan nodded, took in a breath, and then raked a hand over his mussed hair. "Sorry. I woke up and you weren't in the office."

"I *was* in the office for two hours," she said. "I didn't want to wake you so I came out here to talk to Mr. Henderson and assure him that I'm safe and then I took a break."

"Don't do that again."

"What, go to the bathroom? That might be hard considering all the coffee I've been consuming."

"You know what I mean. Don't let me sleep."

Putting a hand on his arm, she said, "Nathan, you needed to sleep. It's daylight with bright sunshine everywhere. I think we're safe for now."

"These people don't care about daylight," he said, pulling away.

"I should take my boss up on his offer to come to his estate near Philadelphia. Talk about security." Alisha's boots clicked against the wooden floor, right on his heel. "Because I shouldn't have called you. You'll take this on and work yourself into a frenzy while you shadow me like a guard dog."

"You've got that right," he said, whirling so fast he had to catch her with his hands on her arms to keep from knocking her down. Holding her there, he stared into her eyes while memories filled his head. Sweet memories of summer nights and the wind lifting her hair. Nathan didn't want to let go—of her or the memories. But he shifted back, accepting that they'd been young and full of idealistic dreams back then. Things had changed so much since that sweet summer.

"I'm okay," she said, lifting away to move past him in a quick rush. "I'll be all right, Nathan. Please don't make a fuss. Let's just do our jobs."

"Is that a hint to back off?"

"Not a hint. A request. We have to remain professional and focus on this case. You have to trust me."

"I do trust you, but I also need to make sure nothing happens to you."

She went behind the big desk and sank down into the chair. "Nothing is going to happen," she said. "I hope that with all my heart and I'm thankful that you're willing to drop everything to help me. But you can't panic every time I leave a room."

"Okay, all right," he said through a breath. "I was tired and I woke up in a different place. Don't make any rash decisions about going back to the city. That's the last place you need to be and I don't care what your boss thinks."

"Well, that's understandable because you're tired, same as me. I don't want to seem ungrateful for what you've done for me but I have another option at least. I was in a panic last night."

"You had to be to call me," he said, wishing he could be the first person she called instead of the last.

"I'm better now and regretting that I dragged you into this. But you're allowed to get some rest even if it's on the office couch."

"Sorry," he said. "Waking up like that is part of my job since I move around so much."

He wouldn't tell her that he woke in hotel rooms a lot but this was different. Hotel rooms were impersonal and sterile to the point of being boring. This house, which was now a community center, still held the charm and homey feeling that he remembered so well. Being here again brought it all back, the many hours he'd spent with Alisha, walking the grounds, falling in love and trying to figure out his future. A future he'd hoped to have with her. He'd never imagined that summer so long ago, that being with her would change his life forever in both good and bad ways.

"I understand." Her green eyes softened. Was she remembering, too? "Do you ever stop thinking about her?"

"Who?"

Alisha's eyes held his for a few ticking seconds. "Hannah."

Nathan's heart lurched each time he heard his sister's name. But hearing Alisha say it with a quiet reverence almost did him in. So he turned sarcastic. "No. Never."

"That's what I thought," Alisha said. "I think about her a lot, too, especially around the holidays."

"Can we change the subject?" he snapped, wishing he could wipe some of his memories away. Then because she looked so crushed and her cheeks blushed a bright pink, he added, "It's still hard, Alisha. I'm sorry."

Alisha nodded and studied the notes in front of her. "All the more reason to remember why we need to keep at this and get it over with."

"Agreed," he said, wanting to fight with her some more. But he couldn't bring himself to do that. She blamed herself for Hannah's disappearance and death, same as he did. But it wasn't her fault.

He was solely to blame for his little sister leaving the house that stormy summer day. Hannah had gone looking for him. She'd gotten lost and…

Closing his eyes, he tried to get the image of his sister calling after him out of his head and instead focused on Alisha and her open laptop. "What have you got?"

"I found the names of the victims," she said. "Joshua and Tiffany West."

"Hmm. Common names. Could be aliases."

"You don't trust anyone, do you?"

"I've had too many Tiffanys in my life."

"Oh, really?"

"Here and there."

"I'd say more here than there. Do you date a lot, Nathan?"

"Here and there. Jealous?"

"Nope. Just curious."

"What about you? Got anyone special in your life?"

"*That* is *neither* here *nor* there," she retorted, her tone telling him she could be a tad bitter about any love connections.

He thought of her briefcase and how she carried it like a shield. Same as him, she was married to her work. They both wore the armor of indifference to hide the brutality of being hurt.

Back to business. "What else did you find?"

"Well, they live in an upscale part of the city in a new development. A modern condo in a building that went up about eight months ago. Comps sell for a million and over."

"How did you find out all of this while I slept?"

"I have my sources, PI Craig, same as you. My firm has been more than willing to help. As I said, Mr. Henderson had offered me protection, too."

Her firm would have investigators. "Probably not as good as me, though."

"They found the information I needed and during a holiday week at that."

"Touché," he said, admiring her determination. "Anything else I need to know?"

"Mitchell Henderson recognized the West couple, told me he'd been at a fund-raiser or two where they'd been top donors. He claims they like to flash their money."

She studied the screen and then let out a gasp. "Dr. and Mrs. Joshua West. He has a family practice and—this is interesting—she's a pharmaceutical sales rep, which my boss failed to mention. That explains the fancy sports car and all the shopping bags."

"Those things didn't save them," he replied.

"No, but their lifestyle might have something to do with the way they died. I mean, a doctor and a big pharma rep. Are you thinking what I'm thinking?"

"Illegal drugs? Now who's not trusting?"

"Look, we know it had to be a professional hit," she reminded him. "I'm trying to get a report from the crime scene but my connections only go so far."

"So *now* you need me around," he teased, a sense of relief washing over him. He needed to be needed to keep from going to that dark place that kept him up at night.

"Yes, now you can make yourself useful." Her smile softened the edge. "Do what you do best—get to the truth."

"Is that what I do?" He felt the glow of her praise even if she might be sarcastic.

"You do." She nodded and placed her elbows on the desk then cupped her hands together to rest her chin on them while she stared over at him. "And for once, I don't care what nefarious methods you use."

"I have friends in high places," he said. "And some in low places. Let me make some calls and call in some favors. Maybe we can put our own case file together soon." Then he added, "If you think the FBI will get involved, you must believe this wasn't random."

She closed her eyes for a moment. "No. It felt deliberate. Like a professional hit."

Nathan couldn't argue with that. "If that's the case, this could go way beyond just protecting you. You'll be questioned by everyone from Campton Creek police to the state police and the Philly police. And probably the DEA."

"Yes," she said. "I'll tell them everything I witnessed. I just need to get there from here."

"Yes, because we can only hide you for so long."

Giving him that lifted-chin attitude, she said, "I'll do whatever needs to be done to find these killers."

"That's what I thought," he said with a grim smile.

She gave him a grim smile back. "Meantime, I'll go and find us some lunch."

"So far, so good," he replied watching her walk out into the hallway. "Be aware."

She turned at the door. "Always."

Nathan marveled at her calm nature. But then Alisha had always had a good head on her shoulders and a sense for doing the right thing. That's why she'd walked away from him.

A flash came through the window, causing Nathan to reach for his gun and rush to the hallway door. Grabbing her, he said, "Get down."

Alisha crouched with him as he guided her into the hallway. Nathan held a hand on her back and whispered, "Get in the powder room and lock the door."

"My phone—"

"No time. Now."

She did as he told her while he slipped to the front window and peeked out. No one. Nathan circled to the portico door and keyed the code to open it. After slipping out, he reset the code to lock the door behind him.

Broad daylight and someone was already messing with them.

This situation would not go away until they did something about it.

Easing through the shaded portico, he felt the chill of the day in spite of the sun. When he heard a noise near the west side of the garage, Nathan skirted some old-root camellias and slid up against the house. Then he did a quick glance around the corner and spotted a man with a huge camera.

A reporter or someone who needed to prove she was alive and hiding here?

The news of the murders had been all over the papers, television news and online sources. Someone must have gotten Alisha's name. He'd take care of this intruder.

"Hey," he called as he climbed out of the camellias with his gun in plain sight. "What are you doing?"

The man jeered at him. "I'm just doing my job. Heard a woman staying here might have some information on those murders in Philadelphia the other night."

"You heard wrong. No one here to talk to you."

The scruffy man came close, his beard and hat covering most of his face. Nathan studied him. He looked disheveled and his posture held an edge that reeked of someone posing as a photographer.

Nathan didn't waste any time. The man gave him a quick glance and made his move, lifting the camera in the air to strike at the same time Nathan grabbed him with one hand and pushed him up against the side of the brick home, causing the camera to fall into the bushes. Placing his handgun against the man's ribs, he said, "I suggest you tell me who you really are and who sent you here."

Alisha came out of the powder room and ran to the office to find her phone. She pulled on her heavy sweater and dropped the phone in the pocket. After searching the room, she grabbed a small porcelain statuette that was probably worth more than a week's salary. But it would make a good weapon.

After searching all the rooms downstairs, she came back to the stairs and crossed over to the carriage house, keying in the code for the door to open.

"Granny?"

"We're right here, Alisha."

She sighed and rushed inside the sitting room to find her grandmother and Mrs. Campton working on a Christmas-inspired jigsaw puzzle. "Are you two all right?"

"Why wouldn't we be?" Miss Judy asked, her elegant eyebrows lifting. "We've both had some soup and it's about time for our afternoon naps. You should rest, too. You look exhausted."

"Did you hear any noises? See a camera flashing?"

"We don't hear very well," her grandmother pointed out. "And we have the drapes shut to stay warm."

"Good," Alisha said, hurrying to the window. Then she saw an official-looking SUV, lights flashing, as it turned into the drive up to the house.

"Now I see something flashing," Miss Judy said, pointing to where Alisha stood. "Do we have company?"

"The state police," Alisha replied. "And Nathan's dragging a man toward the vehicle. I'd better go down."

"No, young lady, you stay right here with us," her grandmother admonished. "Whoever's intruding on our property shouldn't see you here. He might think you're here, but he doesn't need to verify that fact."

Impressed with her spry grandmother's way of thinking, she said, "I think he already knows I'm here." She watched as Nathan shoved the man toward Deputy Benton. "His camera flash alerted us. I guess Nathan found him and obviously called the police."

"You should let Nathan know you're with us," Granny said, nodding. "He'll worry if he can't find you."

Remembering how concerned he'd been this morning, Alisha nodded. "Good idea."

Alisha texted Nathan: *I'm with Granny and Mrs. C. We are all safe in the carriage house.*

She watched and waited. He tugged at his phone, read her text then turned to the window. Without showing her face, she quickly put her hand out, waved then stepped back. He'd be mad at her. Again.

That seemed to be the only relationship they had right now. One annoyed with the other, it usually involved him breaking the rules while she tried to abide by the law.

But she also knew that Nathan was an honest, good man who'd do anything to help someone in need. Even her.

"Everything okay?" Mrs. Campton asked in her serene way.

"Apparently, the intruder has been neutralized and is now taking a ride in an official SUV," Alisha replied. "Mind if I wait here for Nathan? I was supposed to stay locked in the powder room."

Her grandmother stood and tugged her close. "I'd feel better if you stayed right here, but the powder room was a good plan."

"He won't like me leaving the powder room. He tells me to stay put but I can't do that when people are prowling around."

"Men consider it their duty to protect the women they care about," Miss Judy said with that same serenity she'd always held.

Alisha stood back and stared at both of them, her

heart bursting with love and a bit of bittersweet regret. "How did you both do it?"

"Do what?" Granny asked, her expression puzzled but pleased.

"Love the same man all of your life."

Her grandmother glanced at Miss Judy, their eyes holding some sort of secret message.

"Oh, that's easy," Miss Judy said with a smile. "It was our duty to protect them, too, in our own way, which is with prayer and understanding and by trying to meet them halfway in compromise. But mostly, we stayed with our husbands out of love. That's what commitment is all about—we love through the hard times and love through the pain and anger. Love conquers all."

Alisha didn't know how to respond to that. She wanted to believe those words, however. "Wow. That's amazing."

"That's life, darling," Miss Judy said. Then she slipped in a piece of the puzzle. "Aha! That piece has been nagging me all day!"

Alisha smiled and shrugged. "I think that's my problem. I feel like pieces of my puzzle are missing."

"You just have to find the right fit." Judy shrugged back with a giggle.

"I'll make you some tea," Granny said. "And I'm guessing you haven't had lunch."

Alisha relaxed in spite of her worries. "That sounds nice, Granny."

She couldn't confess, but each time Nathan ran out that door to protect her she worried fiercely for his safety and she remembered how much she'd loved him once.

Did that mean she was doing her duty to him?

SEVEN

"So our roaming photographer isn't talking much," Carson told Alisha and Nathan later that day while they sat huddled in the office. "Word is getting out, no matter that the authorities are keeping this on the down-low. People will figure out that Alisha is alive and well and hiding out in Campton Creek."

"Here's what we know about the man the police took away this morning," Nathan said, thinking they'd have to do this one step at a time. The newshounds smelled a good story and they'd want to interview the only eyewitness to these murders, even if it put that witness in danger.

Alisha lifted her chin, ready to do battle. "Tell me everything."

"Corey Cooper. He actually is a reporter-photographer, but his shady tactics have given him a pretty impressive rap sheet—petty stuff such as trespassing on private property, breaking and entering and one assault charge since he's become aggressive in doing his job."

"Well, now he's got an even more impressive rap sheet," Carson noted. "Trespassing and another near assault—on you."

Alisha shook her head. "I guess he'd make money

getting a scoop on the unidentified witness everyone wants to talk to—and that would be me."

"He's been fired several times over," Nathan continued. "Now he's freelance and struggling, desperate. Says the person who hired him left a big wad of money in a safety deposit box at a bank in Philadelphia. The Philadelphia police are checking into the bank since a manager had to give him access per the client."

"So he won't talk because he doesn't know who hired him?" Alisha asked.

"Or he won't talk because he *does* know who hired him and he's afraid he'll be next on the hit list," Nathan replied, still sore that she'd left the powder room. He decided there was no point in telling this woman what to do. She'd always been independent and stubborn.

"Probably the latter," Carson said, nodding. "They'd need proof that you're here. Hiring a somewhat experienced reporter known for snooping on his own allows them to keep their identity a secret." He stood and gave them both a stern glance. "You two stay out of trouble. I'll check on you later today."

"Thank you," Alisha said, her gaze touching on Nathan. "I'm worried about Mrs. C and my grandmother but they seem to be taking all of this excitement in stride."

"A formidable pair," Carson said. "Those two are solid in their faith."

Nathan didn't voice what he was thinking. His parents were solid in their faith, too, but that had not brought his sister back. Nathan couldn't accept that Hannah's unsolved death was the will of God. Now he was being overprotective with Alisha. But the thought of something happening to her gave him chills.

Alisha watched him as if she knew his every thought.

"I don't want to continue this—putting them in danger. These people are vicious."

"You're still in the best place possible," Nathan said, meaning it. "Strangers tend to stand out around here and news travels fast. Even though no one has identified you publicly and most people don't know you're here, I'm sure the whole town is on the watch whether we realize it or not. The shooting has been reported all across the state and we have an officer dead and one in the hospital because of this. Not to mention a car that went over a ravine not far from here."

"Anyone can trace the license plate back to me." Alisha shook her head. "This is such a mess. I should go into hiding somewhere far away from here."

"You know they'll find you," Nathan said. "Look, this place is a stronghold. Carson's gone out of his way to help and the state police have agreed to place officers around the property. And… I'm here. I won't let you go out there alone."

Her twisted frown and straight-out stare indicated frustration but her eyes held apprehension. Both echoes of how Nathan felt but he wouldn't tell her that. Of course, he'd shown her *his* apprehension over and over. No wonder she was ready to bolt.

"I have to go," Carson said. "I do have regular duties to carry out."

Nathan walked with him to the door. "We'll compare notes later."

After Carson left, he turned to find Alisha staring at him with that stern expression on her heart-shaped face. "What?"

She lifted away from the door jamb. "Are you and Carson telling me everything?"

"Of course. You've been right here the whole time we've talked."

"But you two have a thing."

"A thing?"

"Yes. He goes out of his way to help you, even so far as sharing the details of an open, active case."

"A lot of law enforcement personnel share with private detectives and investigators. It's how we get things done."

"I understand but how did you two become friends?"

Chafing under her scrutiny, Nathan moved past her and back into the office. "I knew him growing up and then when I left Campton Creek, he was one of the few people I stayed in touch with. He suggested I become a private investigator."

"Because you were born to do that or because you feel the need to help others find their loved ones? So they won't have to go through what your family did?"

So she wanted to get to the core of what drove him and made him tick? He didn't want to bring up Hannah's death. "A little of both, I think. And I don't want to talk about that."

"*That* is like the elephant in the room, Nathan."

"It doesn't concern you."

"Right. Hannah will always concern me."

"No," he said, anger washing over him. "She is not *your* concern."

"But I was part of the problem that night."

"I tried to tell you then and now—I don't blame you for what happened to Hannah."

"But Nathan, you blamed me when you came to me in the park after...after they'd found her. You said we should have never been together that night."

Shaking his head, he stood silent before responding. "I was angry at the world. I didn't handle any of it very well." His expression softening, he added, "I wish I could take back what I said to you but...maybe things worked out for the best with us."

"Then why won't you talk to me? Be honest with me."

He couldn't do this. Not now when he was already antsy and wired. "Alisha, let it go, okay? She's gone. I can't change that."

"So you do still blame me."

He didn't want her to keep thinking anything was her fault. Hannah's death was on him and they both knew it. "I'm the one to blame. Me, alone. She would have never run out into a storm that night if I hadn't left. And we need to get back to trying to figure out who's trying to kill you. That's my priority right now."

"I wish I'd never called you."

"Well, you did and now you're stuck with me, so that line is getting old."

They had a stare-down right there, just inches between them but so much distance, Nathan knew they'd never reach a peaceful compromise.

He'd keep her alive and then he'd be out of her life again. This time for good.

Two hours later, Alisha pulled the last of the sugar cookies out of the oven. "Okay, Granny, this batch makes six dozen cookies. I hope that's enough for the baskets we're putting together."

Frazzled from searching for answers on the two men who were now wanted by the law, she'd offered to help her grandmother make cookies. The reprieve had cleared her head, at least.

"Plenty, darling," her grandmother replied. "Why don't you make us some Christmas tea while these finish cooling? Then we'll ice them and hopefully we can deliver them tomorrow."

The kitchen smelled of sugar and spice, the familiar scents making Alisha wish this was an ordinary day during the Christmas season. A day where she could go for a walk near the creek or stroll through one of the garden trails.

Alisha wanted to help deliver the cookies, but Nathan had warned her she needed to stay hidden here on the estate. Growing up, she'd always enjoyed baking and decorating Christmas cookies and then going on the deliveries afterward. Her grandmother knew a lot of people within the Amish community so they'd bundle up and head out in Granny's sturdy station wagon and go door-to-door visiting with several of the Amish families, Miss Judy all warm and cozy in the back seat. They'd come home with baked goods and handmade trinkets from their Amish friends.

The first time she'd ever seen Nathan had been during one of those deliveries. A senior in high school, she'd been fascinated with the Amish for a long time. Her parents didn't like coming here much, called it country and boring, but Alisha loved the quietness of this quaint village and the history behind it even if her mother, who'd been raised here, resented it. Charlotte Willis Braxton, married to a successful Boston lawyer and herself a tenured professor, loved the big city and her society friends but Alisha loved Campton Creek.

One smile from Nathan and she'd become even more intrigued with the Amish. He might have jumped the fence but when he smiled now, she saw that rugged, handsome boy who'd taken her heart over a basket of freshly baked cookies.

Pushing away that memory and those of the summer

afterward, when she and Nathan met again and became so close that they fell in love, she thought about the faith and strength in this community.

Admiral Edward Campton Senior's grandfather had owned most of the land on both sides of the winding creek that deepened near the big covered bridge in the middle of the community. When an Amish couple with six hungry children had knocked on the door of Campton House one cold winter, Mr. Campton had invited them in and his wife had fed them and then they'd let the family stay in their home until they could make arrangements for them.

That led to the couple moving into another home the Camptons owned—their original farmhouse. The couple worked the land and helped them around the estate to pay them back. Mr. Campton gifted them with the land and the rental house so the Amish family could stay. Then word got out.

Soon, he was selling off land to the Amish until all he had left was the estate grounds. The story went that Grandfather Campton could never turn down anyone in need and that the Amish around here had stayed by his side until the day he died. Then they'd helped his widow and now Miss Judy after the Admiral died. When the Campton's only son Edward Junior, a navy SEAL, had died in combat, the Amish had been the first to show up and organize everything while they grieved.

Alisha had looked forward to this week, but now she was back under the worst of circumstances.

The teakettle whistled rudely, bringing her out of her memories. Alisha made two cups of tea and found her grandmother in the little sitting room with two iced tree-shaped cookies.

"There you are," Granny said. "Let's enjoy the fruits

of our labor. And while we're at it, let's talk about what's going on."

Alisha sat down in the cushioned chair beside the sofa. "A murder case. Not what I wanted to bring for Christmas."

"I know all about that horrible incident," Granny replied, her eyes warm and knowing. "I'm sure the authorities will find these evil people. I'm more concerned about you."

"I'll be okay," Alisha said, wanting to reassure her grandmother. "I'm being careful and alert and we have people watching out for all of us."

"I mean you and Nathan."

"Oh." Alisha glanced over at her grandmother. "Do you think I was wrong to turn to him?"

"No, I'm thankful that you called on Nathan for help."

"Then what are you fretting about?"

"I know how intense things got with you two long ago. Your mother might not ever forgive either of us for that."

"Mom knows how to hold a grudge but I can't change that," Alisha said. "It ended and... I have a good life now."

"But you're alone and so is he."

"And that's the way it has to be for now, Granny. You aren't suggesting that Nathan and I—"

"Get back together?" Her prim grandmother looked a tad too guilty. "The thought did cross my mind. He's no longer Amish and you're still single."

Alisha shook her head. "I'm sorry but that can't happen. We're two very different people now. I have my work and...he lives for his work."

"Work isn't life, darling."

"But it's all I have."

Alisha put a hand to her mouth. "You managed to force that confession right out of me and with a cookie to bribe me."

Bettye laughed. "I suppose I did at that." Putting down her china teacup, she took Alisha's hand in hers. "I'm so proud of you but I want you to be happy. Not just content. But truly happy the way your grandfather and I were."

Alisha had long ago given up on that kind of happiness. "So you never regretted leaving your family?"

Granny stared across the room to the one card she'd received early on from her mother, telling her that she would always love her. She'd framed that card, a beautiful sketching of Amish country in Ohio. "I regret nothing. I've missed them, no doubt, and we did finally reach out to each other and I've kept in touch enough to attend funerals and send Christmas cards, but I knew I belonged with your grandfather and so, no, I've never regretted that. I loved him enough to leave everything else behind."

Alisha could see that love in her grandmother's eyes. "I think that might be the problem with Nathan and me, Granny. He loved his sister and now she's dead. He thinks he'd not worth anyone's love. And he sure doesn't want to be with me, especially when I'm partially to blame."

Granny shook her head. "No, ma'am, you are not to blame and neither is Nathan. *Gott*'s will."

Alisha couldn't accept that. "So God wanted Nathan's family to suffer and automatically accept Hannah's death and then just move on?"

"No, God knows their anguish and he knows their strength. But we can't question the ways of the Lord. There is a reason for everything. I know your analytical brain can't quite accept faith the way I do, but I also know that you depend on the Lord same as me."

"I do depend on God because you taught me that and I pray every day that Nathan can get over Hannah's death and finally find some peace in his life. He's always out there searching, trying to help others. But why can't he heal and move on with his own life?"

The door to the apartment slammed, causing Alisha to come out of her chair and whirl around.

Nathan stood there staring at her with such anger she actually took a step back. "What business is it of yours whether I find any peace of not?" he asked. "You don't know me anymore and you certainly don't need to waste your prayers on me. What *you* should do is let go of that heavy blame *you* want to keep. You have no part in this."

EIGHT

"Nathan."

He turned and whirled back to the door. Alisha glanced at her grandmother. "What should I do?"

"Go talk to him," Granny said, nodding, her tone solemn.

Alisha grabbed a wool wrap, hurried across the breezeway and spotted him out in the back garden, staring off toward the water beyond the trees. Without thinking, she ran into the big house and hurried down the stairs toward the sunroom. When she opened the French doors out onto the terrace, a burst of cold, late-day air greeted her, pricking at her eyes and causing them to water.

Or maybe she was crying real tears for the man who stood hunched over, his hands in the pocket of his jeans. How long would he carry this burden?

As she drew closer, she called out. "Nathan?"

He pivoted, the anger she'd heard in his voice still smoldering in his eyes. Stalking toward her, he stopped a few feet away. "You shouldn't be out here."

"I'm worried about you," she said, a cold mist of breath heaving into the air. "Come back inside by the fire."

He didn't move. He scanned the trees and woods. "I needed some air. And you need to get back inside."

"No, I'm not going in without you. You're exhausted and you need food and rest—not just coffee."

"Don't tell me what I need, Alisha."

"Then don't pretend you don't care. I know what you heard in there hurt you and I'm sorry."

"You've been sorry for a long time now, but I've tried to tell you this is not your burden to bear."

"This burden," she said, advancing toward him, "is all about your need to be a martyr because of Hannah. For Hannah. That's why you left, right? You decided on your own that you were no longer worthy of being Amish. And you decided you no longer wanted to be with me."

Lifting her hand out to make her point, she added, "Have you ever considered how arrogant that is? That you get to suffer but no one else is allowed, that you won't try to turn this grief over to God and let Him help you to heal. We get through these things because our faith gives us strength. And yet, you push everyone away when you could let all of us help you."

"That's right. I decided. End of discussion. You don't get to suffer along with me."

Alisha stopped short and drew back. "What did you say?"

"I said—"

A shot rang out, echoing through the woods and causing the forest animals down by the creek to scurry into action. Nathan dived for Alisha, knocking her to the ground near an arbor with a leafless vine covering it.

"Are you hit?" he asked, his anxious gaze sliding over her face.

"No, I'm all right," she said, too numb to even feel a bullet. "What do we do now?"

He glanced up and then back toward the woods. "A sniper near the water. I told you to go inside."

"I wanted to talk to you."

Another shot hit one of the arbor posts, nicking the wood into splinters that rained down on their heads.

He didn't fuss at her anymore. "We need to find shelter. I don't have my weapon."

Alisha glanced around, checking to make sure her grandmother wasn't peeking out the back window. Then she spotted the sunroom door. "I left the door cracked."

Nathan looked into her eyes. "I'm going to move over and I want you to crawl into the arbor and get behind one of the chairs."

"What about you?"

"Don't worry about me."

Like asking her not to breathe. She'd been worrying about him since the night he'd told her he was leaving Campton Creek. Without her.

"I told you I'm not going back inside without you," she reminded him.

"Stop being so stubborn and do as I'm asking," he replied, a soft plea in his words.

Alisha didn't want to add to their troubles by being stubborn, so she caved. If she did get in the house, she could call for help, at least. "Okay, but…don't get shot."

She knew he wouldn't care if he took a bullet, but she sure would. Admitting that gave her courage. "Okay, let me up and I'll hide over by the table and chairs."

Nathan nodded and lifted up to squint into the sunny woods. "I see a glint. Could be our man. To the east near that big oak tree."

"I'll take your word for it," Alisha said, afraid to move.

"Are you ready?"

"Yes."

Nathan gave her one last look, his hand briefly touching her cheek as he did a drop-and-roll. Alisha did the same, flipping over to crawl toward the shelter of the old arbor, her wrap caught against her skin and the rocky dirt, tearing, holding her back. Thankfully the chairs underneath were tightly woven black metal, a slight source of protection.

Another shot rang out and Nathan crouched down and ran toward her. "We're pinned in and I don't have my phone."

"I didn't bring mine," Alisha said. "Only open air between us and that door." She shivered, grabbed at her tattered wrap. It was ruined but still warm.

Nathan scooted closer and tugged her into his arms. "I've got you, Alisha. No matter what, you need to remember that."

Huddled in the safety of his arms, Alisha prayed for this brave, tortured man. He'd been in her peripheral vision since she'd been eighteen. But now she was beginning to see him straight on and clearly.

Touching her fingers to his jaw, she said, "I've got you, too. You need to remember that."

The darkness in his eyes shifted and lightened, a brief shard of clarity shining through as he gazed into her eyes.

And her heart was remembering why she'd fallen for him in the first place.

"Nathan, I—"

Another shot hit the still, cold air. The bullet ricocheted off one of the old chairs and pinged into the shrubbery behind them.

"Not a trained sniper or we'd both be dead. But close enough to hit one of us if he doesn't let up," Nathan said.

Then something happened that had both of them sitting up to take notice.

The sunroom door flew back, and her grandmother stood with a high-powered rifle, her eyes, bifocals in place, set against the scope. Bettye stood perfectly still, aimed and fired at least three rounds into the woods.

Alisha heard her grandmother calling, "Run. Hurry. I'll cover you."

They ran quickly, staying against the shrubbery until they were close to the open door. Bettye backed away but kept the rifle in sight of the woods. She kept firing until they were through the door. While they collapsed against the floral porch couch, Granny sent out one more volley and then closed the door with such a proper ladylike slam, they both started laughing.

"Granny, where did you learn to shoot like that?"

"From me," came the voice from behind them. They looked back into the parlor and saw Judy Campton in her wheelchair, a slick pistol centered on her lap.

"I will never forget what I witnessed here today," Nathan said to Alisha.

They sat at the kitchen table, safe and warm, while two officers combed the woods for shell casings and worked on a grid of the yard, hoping they could find bullets to turn over to ballistics. The shooter was long gone, leaving only some muddy footprints by the creek.

After talking to the officers on the scene, Carson told them to stay in for the rest of the day. Alisha had chosen to remain close to her grandmother, so Nathan followed her and here they sat, eating supper and waiting.

At least they had something interesting to talk about.

"So Mrs. Campton and you learned how to shoot to protect yourselves?" Alisha asked, her tone telling Nathan that she was still shocked. Shocked about the whole episode and about his remarks to her, too, probably.

"I actually learned how growing up Amish," Bettye explained. "But Judy and I have perfected the art."

"So you practiced through the years?" Alisha asked.

"Obviously," Judy said with a serene smile. "I taught her a few tricks I learned from the Admiral."

Bettye laughed and shook her head. "Girls aren't supposed to be interested in guns but I watched and listened whenever my *daed* and brothers would sit cleaning their hunting weapons. They used them to hunt or to scare off predators."

Nathan shot Alisha a quick smile. He was still angry at her but he'd cooled his jets so he could keep his head in the game. He hadn't meant to hurt her earlier but some things needed to be left unsaid. Her accusations against him still stung. How was he supposed to get over his sister's death when he was reminded about Hannah each time his phone rang, each time he had to tell another family that their loved one wasn't returning?

He'd found a lot of people safe and sound but he'd also discovered a few who were dead and gone. It never got easier and he never found any relief. Was he being too self-righteous by refusing to let go of his grief? Should he depend more on God and less on his own tormented assumptions?

He couldn't think about that right now.

"But you never used a gun?" he asked Bettye while they tried to enjoy the meal she and Mrs. Campton had insisting on preparing.

"I had to learn the hard way one day when all the menfolk were in town loading up supplies for the spring plantings. A big snake showed up out near the barn. I think it was a timber rattlesnake. Scared my poor *mamm* almost to death."

"You shot the snake?" Alisha asked, a buttered roll in her hand.

"I tried. Missed the first couple of times but then I remembered how calm my *daed* would be when he held a gun to shoot an animal or a varmint." She gave a dainty shrug. "So I calmed down, aimed and boom, that snake lived no more."

"Your grandmother is a remarkable woman," Mrs. Campton added with a smile. "After they heard that story when we were all still so young, my sailor and your granddaddy got it in their heads they'd take us to target practice in case we ever needed to use a weapon."

"I haven't fired a rifle in years," Granny said, shaking her head.

"Well, today, you did just that," Mrs. Campton said. "Good thing we kept up the practice as long as we did."

"Yes, good thing." Nathan finished the baked chicken and mashed potatoes and stood. "Ladies, thank you for the food. But I need to go and see what the law found out there today."

Alisha glanced up at him. "I'm going to stay here and help clean the table. I'll talk to you later."

He nodded, the moment of silence between them shouting too loudly while the two Annie Oakleys gave each other speaking looks.

Excusing himself, he turned and left before they forced him to eat a piece of coconut cake. The food was great and being pampered reminded him of home, but Nathan knew in his heart he had to control all of these sentimental feelings coursing through his system. He'd find these killers and then he'd be on his way, on to the next case. Finding people was his thing.

What if he couldn't find the murderers, though? Would Alisha have to spend the rest of her life with this threat hanging over her head? She already blamed herself for what had happened to Hannah.

That's partly your fault.

His memories of the past suddenly shouted loud and clear.

"I shouldn't be here with you, Alisha. I should have stayed with my family. Hannah is gone and now I've lost everything."

Nathan could never forget the shattered look in her misty eyes nor the pain and shame he'd seen on her face as they stood in the park one last time.

"You still have me, Nathan."

"No, I can't be with you now. Not like this."

She'd started crying but she didn't beg him to stay. No, Alisha took matters into her own hands. "Then you won't have me in your life anymore. I won't be a reminder of what has happened. I can't live with your resentment."

With that, she'd turned and ran back toward Campton House. He had not seen her again until a couple years ago when the Admiral had died and Mrs. Campton had invited Nathan to the dedication of Campton House as a community center.

If he could take it all back…

He'd said some awful things that night after they'd heard Hannah was found dead. Lashing out at Alisha had made sense at the time but he'd regretted it a thousand times over.

And today, he'd said another horrible thing to her. He didn't want to share this burden, this torment. He'd held it around his heart like an armor of shame. He *had* become a martyr of sorts, pushing away the world he'd so longed to be a part of and shutting out those who loved him the most.

When would he stop punishing himself?

And her?

Nathan texted Carson and told him he'd be in the office.

A knock at the front door brought Nathan out of his dark thoughts.

Carson came in, the cold blasting behind him. "More snow tonight so I hope the bullets and casings they found will provide something to work with."

"But no sign of the shooter?"

"Nah. He must have taken a rowboat up the creek to get here. Then once he was fired on, he had to have jumped in the boat and paddled away to hide out somewhere across the shore. They went around to search and ask if anyone had seen him. Got nothing. But several people did hear the shooting."

"Yes, pretty hard not to hear in such a quiet place."

"Look, Nathan, I have a suggestion."

"I'm listening."

"Word will spread and more people will come looking. The press is hot for a grisly story and this one fills the bill."

"So?"

"So, I think you and Alisha should go deeper into hiding."

"And where do you think we should go?"

Carson scratched his head and stared into Nathan's eyes. "The last place a killer would look for you. Amish country."

"We are in Amish country," Nathan pointed out.

"I mean all the way in. Dress the part, play the part, find someone you can trust to hide you."

"The Amish don't condone violence and dishonesty. I won't bring that on this community."

"It's already here."

"And what about Bettye and Mrs. Campton?"

"Those two won't leave but the town police can assign two officers to patrol the grounds day and night." Then he shrugged. "And from what I've heard about today, I'd say the women can hold their own if push comes to shove."

Nathan turned toward the fire and stared at the flames. "Alisha won't like this."

"What won't I like?"

They both looked up to find Alisha standing in the hallway, her eyes full of questions and her expression full of stubbornness.

NINE

"Nathan, what's going on now?"

Alisha saw the look that passed between the two men. "One of you had better start talking."

Nathan scratched his head and turned to her. "We need to go into hiding away from Campton House."

"I couldn't agree more but you both told me this is the safest place for us right now."

"We thought that," Nathan replied, his eyes stormy blue. "But they breached the estate from the water today and they'll find another way in."

"Then what's the plan?" she asked as she stepped close to the fire, her shivers coming from the fear holding her like a clawing hand. "Where are we going?"

Nathan looked uncertain and Carson stared at the floor.

"Carson thinks we should hide in plain sight—within the Amish community."

Alisha's shock returned with a jolt. "What? And put more innocent people in harm's way. I won't do it. I'll go back to Reading and rent a hotel room. Or I'll head straight back to Philadelphia."

"You can't do that, Alisha. They'll track your every move."

"And they won't do that here?"

"Out there, they have a better chance of finding you," Nathan said, his gaze beseeching. "The Amish won't condone violence or danger but they will protect someone in need."

"There has to be a better way," she said. "A safe house somewhere."

"The Amish community is safe," Carson finally said. "If we find the right family and you two can blend in and follow the rules, you should be fine."

"But how will we find the right family?" Alisha paced by the fire, her boots hitting the hardwood floor. "I'm not doing this. It's not right to put a family in jeopardy."

"There is one other option," Nathan said, his eyes on her.

She stared him down while Carson looked confused. "I'm listening."

"I can take you to my cabin."

That halted Alisha in her tracks. "What?"

Carson ran a hand down his five-o'clock shadow. "I don't know—"

Nathan held up his hand to stop both of them. "It's on the fringes of the Amish community, deep in the woods. Few people even know it's there. We can dress to look Amish and sneak out after dark." He nodded to Alisha. "I know you keep Amish clothes here, as needed."

"You know too much," she retorted, the thought of going deep into the woods with this lone wolf scaring her in a different way. "But yes, we have the proper clothing."

Carson put his hands on his hips. "You can't take your vehicle. They might have seen it here before you hid it in the garage."

"We'll walk," Nathan said. "We'll bundle up and keep

to the paths, not the main roads. My cabin sits about three miles from the main road."

"I can find someone to watch near the woods," Carson said. "I know where a deer stand is hidden near your cabin. We can put an off-duty officer there. So no official vehicles will give you away and he can keep watch and alert you by phone if he notices anyone headed that way."

"This is ridiculous," Alisha said. "They can follow us on foot and then we'll have nowhere to hide."

"Do you want to risk another attack here?" Nathan asked.

"No." She didn't want that but she didn't like *this*. They stood staring at each other until she finally let out a sigh. "I'll have to explain to my grandmother."

"You can tell her you're leaving, but don't tell her where you're going," Nathan suggested. "The less she knows, the better."

"I agree." Alisha gave Nathan one last look, her heart in a panic. Would she be able to do this? To run away with the man she'd tried to forget? Once, leaving with Nathan had been her dream. Now she was living a nightmare.

Nathan reached out a hand to her. "You know I wouldn't do this if we had any other choice. I promise I'll protect you and I'll make sure your grandmother and Mrs. Campton are safe."

Carson nodded. "The Amish are getting word that something is brewing but they tend to stay out of matters of the law. They'll keep an eye on Campton House, too. They will warn of anything strange happening."

Alisha pulled away from Nathan and sat down on a chair. "I don't know. I should have never come here in the first place." She let out a breath but held in her tears. "I just needed to see my grandmother."

Nathan bent down on one knee and took her hand again. "I understand. You wanted to feel safe, right?"

"Yes." She stared into his eyes. They were calm now, a deep blue calm that scared her all over again. "I was so frightened and in shock and I wasn't thinking straight."

He kissed her forehead, a brief touch of his lips to her skin. "It's going to be all right."

She savored that sweet gesture. "But you can't be sure, can you?"

His eyes flashed a pain so deep it cut straight to her heart. He was thinking of little Hannah. "No, I can't be sure. But I'm going to do my best to take care of you."

Carson cleared his throat. "What time do you want to leave?"

Nathan stood, his gaze still on Alisha. "Later tonight. At least, the moon isn't full."

Alisha stood. "I'll go and talk to Granny then I'll find some clothes for us."

Nathan lifted his chin in acknowledgement.

Once she was out of the office, Alisha stopped and stared out into the well-lit backyard. The trees and old shrubs she'd always loved now held a sinister, hulking presence. Leaving had to be the only way.

But the people who were after her wouldn't know she'd left. What if they came after her grandmother again?

Whirling back around, she crashed into Nathan and grabbed his arms. "We need to put out the word that I've been placed in a safe house. In the city."

At first, Nathan balked and then realization hit him. "So they'll know you're no longer here?"

"Yes. Exactly. So they'll search for me somewhere else. Do you think Carson can make that happen?"

"He probably can. The locals in Philly might not like it. In all this confusion, I didn't get an opportunity to speak to you alone about something else that came up."

"What?"

"The FBI *is* on the case in Philly but they're being tight-lipped about the whole thing. They'll want to question you just as we thought. But they might also want to put you into protective custody."

"Did the town police tell them where I am?"

"Right now, you're classified as unavailable for questioning but you're willing to cooperate. Carson and Officer Cantor both gave the same statement."

"Right, but Carson's helping *unofficially*," she said, doubt in her eyes. "I don't want to get your friend in trouble. I need to meet with the FBI, but I also need to stay alive to do that."

Nathan nodded and scanned the windows. "They know that, so we'll wait to hear from them."

"But they might show up at the cabin."

"We don't have to tell them where you are. They'll get mad and then they'll get on with the job. We can stall."

"I see you're still good at going to ground."

"Been doing it most of my life."

"I'm too tired to argue," she admitted. "Let me go and explain to Granny, please."

"Do you need backup?"

"No."

She whirled to leave but turned. "Thank you, Nathan."

He nodded, watched her cross the breezeway and then turned as she entered the apartment door.

They were in this thing together now, no matter what. Alisha prayed they'd both come out alive.

Hours later, covered from head to toe, Alisha wearing a dark bonnet and black cloak, Nathan wearing a hat and heavy overcoat, they slipped away into the night.

Nathan kept her between him and the open fields as they followed the forest paths the Amish used to come and go around the country side. He had a small flashlight but only turned it on when the path grew heavy with overgrowth.

Alisha was quiet, allowing him to hold her arm as they hurried through the bitter cold. "Are you all right?" he whispered.

She nodded. "Granny is worried for me but she's brave. She'll pray for us. They are aware of the officers patrolling back and front now and the alarm is set."

"Carson and I checked everything one last time before we left," he said to reassure her.

Alisha stumbled and Nathan caught her against his chest. She felt so small and fragile but he knew the strength encased inside this woman's heart.

Staring up at him, she said, "They kept telling me they'd be fine. Their faith is solid—like a wall. But we both know faith can only carry you so far."

He held her there for a moment, accepting that she hadn't pushed him away, taking in her eyes and how innocent she looked. "Faith carries us all the way through," he replied. "Those two know that no matter what, God's will and their faith will see them to the end."

She did pull back then. "I don't want to prove that faith. I don't want one of them to die even if they are ready for Heaven."

"Don't think that way," Nathan told her as he guided her along. "We have to believe we'll all make it through this."

"I wish you and I could have that assurance. I'm trying."

He held her there. "I'm trying, too. And I'm sorry I got so angry today. Your words made me think about how prideful I am, refusing to turn back to God—I mean all the way back, not just when it's convenient."

Her eyes brightened, the sparse light sparkling through like joy. "Nathan, I'm glad to hear that."

"I guess being back here with your grandmother and you has brought out a lot of pent-up memories. I never gave up on God but I did give up on attending church. I hope He listens to a burned-out man with a chip on his shoulder, sitting on a park bench."

"I'm pretty sure He does," she replied, sending him a hopeful glance. "I hope He listens to a tired law associate who has to burn the midnight oil, even on Sunday mornings."

Nathan smiled at that. "I'm guessing He's listening right now as we head out into the woods on faith alone."

They started walking again, wary but less weary. "Up this way," Nathan said. "We have about a mile to go."

"Does that make my faith weak?" she asked, her voice timid now. "I made that comment about not testing faith."

"What? Because you want your grandmother to live?"

"Yes. Does that make me selfish?"

"No, Alisha. That makes you human."

"I keep thinking if I hadn't stopped there, we'd all be oblivious and safe and enjoying the holidays. I would have heard about the shooting on the news but I could have gone on with my life."

"Stop second-guessing this thing," he gently chastised. "You can't go back and change what happened— you shouldn't have stopped there, you shouldn't have come here, you shouldn't have called me. None of that matters now. We're here and we have to stay one step ahead of these people. Of everything that you think you should or shouldn't have done, coming here was probably the best decision considering the circumstances."

Easy for him to tell her that when he'd been thinking along the same lines for years now.

They heard a noise off to the side.

Nathan guided her to a stand of saplings and held her there against a tree, his heartbeat bumping against hers. Putting a finger to his lips, he gave her a quick glance. Alisha nodded and held to him.

When he saw a huge shadow on the path, Nathan tugged her tightly into his arms. "If something goes wrong, run as fast as you can to the east and look for the Schrock farm."

She bobbed her head, her eyes wide with questions he wasn't ready to answer.

Nathan held her with one hand and placed his other hand on his Beretta. Then he carefully looked around the tree and let out a grunt of relief.

"The big stag. Look. He hangs out in these woods. I've often left him food out my back door."

Alisha peeked over his shoulder and squinted in the scant light from the crescent moon caught between clouds. "Oh, my. He's a beauty."

The stag moved over the forest floor, lifting his head when he caught their scent. He stood majestic and still, the snow falling softly around him.

"A twelve-pointer if I'm seeing right," Nathan replied. "Hard to tell in the dark, but I think he's the one I feed every now and then when I'm home. We've become buddies."

"He's big enough to see us and I'm sure he knows we're intruders."

"Maybe he'll recognize my scent and let us be. He'll run when we make a move."

He took her hand and led her back onto the path, his

small flashlight guiding them. "*As the deer pants for water...*"

"*So my soul longs for you, O God,*" she finished. "Psalm 42."

"Maybe God is giving us a sign."

"Or maybe a deer just crossed our path."

The big animal leaped into the air and crashed off through the forest.

"A sign," Nathan said, thinking he had not looked for signs from the Lord in a long time. But here he was with the one woman he could never get out of his system, trying to protect her, trying to find some sort of redemption. A bad idea or a second chance?

His heart filled with a strange sensation. A sense of peace and home and security. Or maybe he was just cold and tired and seeing things that weren't really there.

But the night sky gave him comfort so he hurried Alisha along toward his tiny cabin. "We'll be there soon."

She gave him a little smile and held out her hand. Nathan accepted it like a lifeline, a thankfulness settling in his heart. Without a word they moved over the quiet snow and came up on the cabin.

"Home," Nathan whispered. Because for the first time in a long time, this place felt like home.

TEN

Alisha stood near the door while Nathan found the light switch. "I do have electricity," he said. "I didn't go totally off the grid."

"That's good to know."

He turned on a small lamp away from the two front windows, probably so no one would notice they were here. "It's not much and I'm not here very often but it'll keep us warm and, hopefully, safe."

"Do you have a security system?" she asked.

"Yes." He held up his Beretta. "This."

"Well, that's reassuring."

"Don't worry. I have good locks on the doors and the windows haven't been opened in years. We'd hear them groaning."

She took in the impressive fireplace and the worn black leather couch and tan-and-black plaid side chair. The room opened into the tiny efficiency kitchen where two more windows held heavy blinds over the sink.

"Has this cabin always been here?"

"Nope. I built it about five years ago."

The man never ceased to amaze her or surprise her. "By hand, I'm guessing."

"Yes. By hand with salvaged logs and lumber. It's solid."

As solid as the man who lived here alone. If he ever actually stayed here. "Do you come here a lot?"

"Only when I'm not on a case, which is pretty much never."

"You should take time, Nathan. Time for yourself."

Giving her a tightly controlled stare, he said, "I'll consider that once I know you're safe."

Alisha didn't push him. The man didn't ever want to talk about his own life. "I feel safe here," she admitted. The little cabin was cozy and homey but a bit spartan.

"The bedroom and bath are over there," he said, pointing to an open door. "I'll take the couch."

"You don't have to do that."

"Yes, I do. I can guard both the front and back doors."

"In that case, yes, I'll be glad to take the bedroom."

He moved around, checking the shadows, adjusting the curtains and blinds. "If you want to change, go ahead. I'll make us some coffee and we can map out a plan."

"A plan?"

"Just in case we have to run again," he said before turning to the stove.

Alisha took off her bonnet and heavy wool cap but left on her apron and dress. "I'm fine in these clothes for now."

Nathan quickly shed his overcoat and turned to stare at her. "Wow. With your hair pulled back and that dark blue dress on, you do look Amish."

"A lot more comfortable than the suits I usually wear," she said, holding out the full skirt. "I have too many clothes so I can appreciate the simplicity of this outfit."

"The Amish are innovative and practical. Nothing is ever wasted."

Alisha stared him down. "You look rather Amish yourself."

"It never actually left my system. Old habits die hard."

He wore a deep blue long-sleeved shirt over brown broad-fall pants and dark laced-up boots. Seeing him dressed this way again brought back a lot of memories for Alisha.

"Those clothes are a little small for you," she noted while he washed the percolator and found a tin of coffee.

How could she ignore the way the shirt fit him too tightly? Nathan had always been handsome but now he held a world-weary attractiveness. She needed to remember they were no longer kids with a crush on each other.

But she also remembered what she'd felt for Nathan so long ago had been more than a crush. After they'd broken up, she'd decided to never let her guard down again. She shouldn't do that now.

He turned, checking on her quietness. "Yep. Not quite my size but at least all Amish clothes are made loose. That helps."

"Yes, my skirt is plenty big." She came out of her stupor and twirled around. "And warm."

Nathan was the quiet one now. His gaze moved over her with a deep warmth. Moving closer, he said, "You look beautiful."

"Thank you." They stalled out on the fashion talk. "Nathan, do you think they'll find us here?"

"I hope not. Carson and one of his men who looks similar to me took my truck to a motel out on the main highway and the police put two plainclothes officers nearby to see who shows. So we'll see if they go looking there first."

Alisha wondered if someone had seen them leaving the estate, but they'd circled back by the creek and crossed over the main covered bridge so it would look like they were walking from a nearby farm. The late hour would be questioned, but if stopped they'd had the excuse of visiting into the night with a sick relative.

"Why did you tell me to run to your father's house if something happened?" she asked, remembering his words from before.

"It's the closest one to this cabin," he explained when he brought over two cups of dark, rich coffee. "Just through the woods, about a half mile beyond the cabin. A narrow path but there. Look for the birdhouses."

He'd always loved building birdhouses. She still had one he'd made for her, a small white house with blue shutters and flowers painted on the sides. He told her a bluebird would live there when they built their house in the woods.

Alisha sat down on the cold leather couch, wanting to know everything about him. "Why did you change your name?"

He placed his coffee mug on the table by the side chair and turned to get a fire going. "Craig is my professional name," he said while he gathered kindling and found matches on the mantel. "I took a professional name to protect my family. I didn't want any of my findings to fall back on them."

"Ah, because sometimes you take on cases such as this one. Dangerous."

"Yes." He studied the growing fire and, satisfied, dusted off his hands and then sat down across from her. "I've brought them enough grief without having someone trying to get to me through them."

"And yet, you built a home nearby and told me to run to them."

"This is an unusual circumstance. I hope it won't come to that."

"Because it involves murder or because it involves me?"

"Both."

Alisha wasn't sure how to respond to his admission. The fire crackled in the quiet, its warmth reaching out to her shivering bones. "I won't say what I'm thinking."

Nathan put down his coffee cup and leaned forward. "I know what you're thinking. You tend to blame yourself for a lot that happens in life."

She couldn't deny that. "Yes, I guess I do. Being an only child can sure put a tremendous pressure on a person. Perfection is hard to achieve and so…guilt takes over."

"So you and your parents still don't see eye-to-eye?"

"No. My dad is mad that I didn't join his law firm right away and my mom is so involved in her teaching and research, she tends to forget I exist. I think I'm one big letdown."

"Your parents are stupid."

She burst out laughing at that. "Well, that or too intelligent for their own good."

"Sometimes intelligent people are the stupidest."

"Duly noted." She finished her coffee. "Let's talk about what we know so far on this case."

"So you're not ready to discuss all of our flaws and dysfunctions?"

She wanted to question him about so many things but Nathan would get the wrong idea and peg her as nosy. "No, are you?"

"Not in the least. Not right now, anyway." He grabbed the small leather overnight bag he'd brought with him. "I have written notes and I've saved some things on my laptop."

"Do we have Wi-Fi?"

He pulled out a heavy oval gadget. "Wireless hotspot. It's charged to last thirty-six hours and there's a tower about ten miles away."

"Always this prepared?"

"It's how I roll," he quipped. "I wind up in some sketchy places at times. But I've managed to get some solid information regarding this case. I have the police report."

"I'm not going to ask how you obtained that so quickly."

"Good, because I won't tell you who helped me."

"I've had my people digging, too." She reached for the briefcase she'd insisted on carrying underneath her cloak. "I printed mine out before we left."

"Smart. We can compare notes." Then he asked, "Have you explained all of this to your firm?"

"Yes. I didn't want my boss to hear about my involvement on the evening news or worry that I'd gone missing. I called the main office and talked to him and then asked for an investigator there to help with some online searches."

Remembering Mitchell Henderson's concern, Alisha knew the senior partner would stand by her. "You keep us posted," he'd said during their conversation. "These people need to be stopped."

He'd questioned her in his lawyerly way, asking for details on the shooter. She gave him what she knew which, beyond a description, wasn't too much.

"Do you trust the people you work with to keep this quiet? They can't reveal where you are."

"Of course." Telling Nathan about her conversation with Mitchell, she nodded. "Why wouldn't I trust them? They know this is a bad situation."

"Because whoever is behind this is ruthless and will

stop at nothing to get to you, including infiltrating your workplace."

"Do you think they'll go after my boss and coworkers?"

"To get to you, possibly. But since you've warned your firm, I hope they're all on the alert."

"Knowing Mr. Henderson, I can almost guarantee that. We have a top-notch security protocol online and on the premises."

"Okay, just needed to check that off my list."

"Thanks. Now I can add worrying about adding the dozens of people who work with me to *my* list."

"Don't. They'd only take that route as a last resort."

He pulled up his phone files while she went through her papers. "So our reporter isn't going to tell us much," Nathan said. "We can only hold him on trespassing but I'm sure he's lawyered up. We need to find out who his lawyer is, to give us a clue."

"Like that will happen."

Alisha studied the paperwork one of the paralegals had sent her earlier. "Hey, I have a list of some of the good doctor's patients. According to what we've found, these are some nefarious people who don't always want to go through proper procedures to get their medications."

"What kind of medications?"

"Opioids," she said, dropping the page she'd been reading. "So a successful doctor who has high-powered and high-paying clients and is willing to write them prescriptions for whatever they need."

Nathan scoffed. "I'd call that a quack."

"But a rich one, according to his bank account. Owns property in Philadelphia, which we've verified, and owns a fancy beach house in the Caymans."

"Of course, the Caymans. Offshore money and all of that. Not to mention a wife who sells pharmaceuticals."

Rubbing a hand down his face, he said, "Let's take the top five on that list and see what we can find."

Alisha got up to find more of the diesel-fuel coffee. She'd be up all night but she couldn't sleep anyway. Searching her briefcase, she found the tin of cookies her grandmother had insisted they bring along and carried it back to the tiny sitting area. "This new information might explain why the FBI is now involved in this case. Philadelphia has a huge opioid problem."

They quickly zoomed on a woman named Andrea Sumter. Nathan read what he'd found. "A widowed socialite with money to burn, travels to the Caymans a lot herself, plenty of photos of her hanging with the Wests at high-society events. Let's keep her high up on the list."

One man on the list was dead. They eliminated two more names. But the last one caught Nathan's attention. "Deke Garrison. Filthy rich. Dirty money. I've heard his name in certain circles."

"Certain bad circles?" she asked, passing the cookie tin.

Nathan took the tin when she offered it and found an oatmeal cookie. "I'd say. You're the only eyewitness, and if he's our man the FBI might already be on this case or they're just snooping, hoping to capture him at last."

"They'll want me to testify if we find these people and bring them to trial. I'll never forget what happened the other night. Those hit men need to go to jail."

"And that's why you're in hiding. We're dealing with dangerous people who've already found you and tried to take both of us out."

She didn't want to think about what would have happened earlier if her feisty grandmother hadn't taken matters into her own hands. "Let's see if we can find out who else the doctor socialized with. He might have kept his drug-trafficking—if that's what he was doing—hidden from his legit friends."The couple I saw shouted rich, entitled and indulgent. Their car, their clothes, their shopping bags said it all."

"And now they can't brag to anyone."

Alisha shivered and then caught herself.

Nathan stood. "Are you cold?"

"No. Just… This is so creepy. I've always dealt in helping people and working with a lot of business contracts, some divorces and some petty criminals. But nothing like this. It's a horror story."

Nathan came and sat down beside her. "Rest," he said, pulling her into his arms. "Just rest."

Alisha knew she should protest but being in his arms again took away all of her horrible memories of the last few days. She felt secure here in this little cabin with Nathan, the fire's warmth lulling her to relax. But this couldn't happen.

She lifted up. "I should go and get some sleep."

"Not yet," he said, his warm breath on her ear, his arms still holding her. "Just let me hold you, okay?" He took an old afghan off the back of the couch and dropped it over her clothes.

Alisha closed her eyes. She needed to get up and move away from him. Too tempting. But sleep took hold of her. Nathan tugged her close so she could lie her head on his shoulder.

She shouldn't feel this safe with him but her limbs felt so heavy and a wave of fatigue moved over her, dragging her down.

"Just for a minute," she said as she drifted off.

Only for a little while.

Nathan woke with a start and glanced around. The fire was out and the room was cold. Alisha lay on the couch, covered in the afghan and another blanket he'd found. She'd fallen asleep almost immediately so he'd lifted her up out of his arms and let her sleep there. He had taken the chair and made do with a pillow and a blanket while he studied the facts they'd gathered.

He'd fallen asleep, his head twisted against the pillow.

Now he was fully awake and hearing things.

A rustling outside brought him out of his chair. Listening, he hurried to the door. It was locked and bolted but that wouldn't stop a killer.

Standing there, he checked his watch. Four o'clock. Nathan found his gun and went to a window to peek out. Maybe the big deer had followed their scent here. Listening, he heard only the wind and the occasional sound of snow falling off of tree limbs.

"What is it?"

He turned to find Alisha sitting up on the couch, her blanket pulled tightly against her.

"False alarm," he said. "Something woke me. Probably an animal passing by."

She didn't look convinced.

"Let me go and check," he said, grabbing his boots and his coat. "You don't go anywhere."

"I won't."

He gave her a questioning stare.

"I do not want to go out there," she said. "I'll make coffee. And you—be careful."

He went out the back and quietly worked his way around the perimeter of the square little cabin. No human prints but lots of animal paw prints. Maybe the raccoon he fed sometimes had returned for a winter treat.

Satisfied, he glanced around the quiet forest and wondered if someone was watching him. The chill took over and he hurried back inside, dusting snow off of his clothes after he closed and locked the door. "All clear. I'll start a fire."

She handed him fresh coffee and headed to the bedroom and stayed there a few minutes. He heard water running so he worked on a quick breakfast. When she returned, she'd changed into sweats and a huge sweater, thick socks covering her feet. Moving toward the fire he'd started, she held her hands out.

"Cold?"

"I might not ever be truly warm again."

He thought about holding her last night and how right it had felt. So right that he'd forced himself away. Then, watching and waiting, he'd fallen asleep in the chair by the fire. And he had the sore neck to prove it.

"We survived the night."

He looked around from where he'd thrown together toast with the freshly baked bread Bettye had packed for them. He had a jar of fresh jam in the pantry. "Yes, we did. So we'll stay hunkered down here and hit hard on piecing this thing together."

"And hope no one interrupts us," she replied, worry sounding in her words, her eyes darting toward the windows.

"Yes."

Nathan kept one ear to the ground while they ate. Because even though he hadn't found any footprints around the cabin, that didn't mean they were safe.

He was pretty sure he'd felt eyes on him when he went out earlier to check. While he watched and waited in here, someone could be doing the very same thing in the woods.

ELEVEN

They spent most of the day going back over what they knew, which wasn't much but every little tidbit painted a picture of what looked like a doctor filtering opioids through his clinic with the help of his so-called pharmaceutical rep wife—the perfect cover. Except one of his dealers must have wanted more money or had found out the good doctor was skimming off the top.

"Everything points to Deke Garrison," he told Alisha after they put together pages of handwritten notes. "He's a patient of Dr. West's, they hung in the same circles and their wives are all over social media together. Parties, vacations, holidays. Tight group. A lot of trips to South America and the Caymans."

Lots of possible scenarios but nothing concrete to go on yet. They didn't have the names of the shooter and driver so Alisha couldn't identify them unless she went back to Philadelphia. The law would expect her to come in and look at mugshots but as far as Nathan was concerned she wouldn't be able to do that with killers after her.

"How do we get to him?" she'd asked when they finally took a break earlier.

"We let the *authorities* take what we have and follow every lead."

"Well, that sure is a change of tune for you, PI Craig."

"I have to work this one by the book," he replied, thinking he had to walk the line to protect her from both the bad guys and a system that would demand everything of her in order to catch these criminals.

Now as night settled over the snow-covered woods and hills, Nathan figured they couldn't stay here indefinitely. Maybe he should get her back to Philadelphia fast and let the authorities there take over. He'd be in a world of trouble for taking her on the run, but what else could he have done?

"You look deep in thought," Alisha said from the kitchen. "Are you okay?"

Nathan got up from his chair and walked over to the small dining table he'd made from scrap wood. "Just pondering our next move."

Alisha motioned to the sandwiches she'd made and the can of soup she'd found in the cabinet. "Peanut butter and jelly with chicken soup. Eat and then we'll talk about what's next."

Nathan rubbed the back of his neck and sat down in one of the old rickety high-backed chairs. Watching her move around this usually solitary kitchen made his heart ache with a pain that seared his soul. He'd long ago given up on love and marriage, or a home other than this one.

He was a self-imposed nomad. He couldn't go through the devastation of losing someone he loved again. The night they'd found Hannah's tiny body by a stream still haunted his dreams. He'd lost her and Alisha both that night. And he'd lost them both because of his own selfish actions. Falling for a girl way out of his league had changed his life and made him realize some men weren't meant to have a family. So he helped other families find their missing loved ones.

That system had worked until now. Now, he'd held Alisha in his arms and realized his heart would never heal. In some ways, the pain was even worse the second time around.

"Nathan?"

He looked up to find her staring at him, concern clear in her gaze.

"What?"

"Is there something you're not telling me?"

"No." He couldn't blurt out what he was thinking. "We need to keep moving. I think tonight." Looking at her clothes, he added, "You need to put your dress back on in case we need to move quickly. Keep your bonnet and cape nearby."

"You think someone is out there, don't you?"

"I haven't seen anyone but my gut says yes."

Surprised, she held her spoon in the air. "And where will we go next?"

He studied her and wished he could keep her here, warm and safe with him for a long time. "Back to Philly."

Dropping the spoon into her soup, she said, "What?"

"We need to get you into the police station so we can look at mugshots. They'll want to talk to you again since we've had several obvious incidents that back up your fears and can prove our case. The best way to get to these people is to start at the beginning. Again."

She sat still and silent, her eyes downcast. "I understand. I can't run forever. I should have gone straight to them in the beginning."

He could tell she was growing weary. "You needed a couple of days to debrief and retreat, to get your head together for what might come."

"Except we've been looking over our shoulders for those two days and endangering everyone around us. You're right. This has to be our next move."

She looked up and into his eyes, her heart shining through. "Granny says things happen for a reason. I want you to know, Nathan, that no matter what, I think we needed this time together. And I hope you'll consider visiting your family during the holidays. We need to put an end to the blame and the guilt and live life to the fullest. For Hannah's sake. That's how we can honor her."

Nathan swallowed the lump in his throat and reached for her hand. So many things he wanted to say but he didn't have the right to need her so much. He wasn't worth her efforts but oh, how he wished he could be worthy of her love again.

They ate their meal in silence and afterward, she went into the bedroom and became Amish again. "I'm ready," she said. Then she went to her briefcase and took out some of her notes and her phone. "Just in case."

Tired, they sat on the couch staring into the fire for what seemed like hours, both too wired to sleep.

"I hate putting you through this," he told her as the night grew late. Taking her into his arms, he said, "Try to rest."

She leaned in, her hand covering his, her eyes telling him what words couldn't say. He wanted to kiss her and hold her and protect her.

"Alisha…"

A snap of a twig outside caused them both to freeze.

And then a hard knock at the door brought him out of his seat and diving for his weapon. He motioned to Alisha and she hurried across the room while he held to what he'd almost said to her before they'd been interrupted.

He wanted Alisha back with him.

* * *

Who would come knocking unannounced here? Alisha wondered, her heart pounding. The only ones who were aware that they were here knew to call or text first. They'd barely gotten settled and now someone was out there. Nathan had suspected this all along. The thought of a standoff here in the woods frightened her but she wasn't going down without a fight.

A light shined outside. She could see it through the slats of the old blinds when Nathan tucked them apart. He looked ready to do battle.

Another knock hit the door.

So now the killer was going to use manners by knocking first?

That gave her time to think.

Alisha rushed to Nathan's side. "Maybe it's a ploy."

"Has to be," he whispered. "Our guard in the woods would have seen them. They must have spotted him first."

Alisha didn't want another law enforcement officer to die because of her. "How do these people find us?"

"They always find a way," he whispered. "I thought we'd bought some time."

"Our time is up," she said. "Do we go out the back?"

Before he could answer, a booming voice shouted. "Nathan Craig? FBI. We know you're in there. Open the door or we'll break it down."

Nathan turned to Alisha. "They might not be FBI," he pointed out. "My gut is telling me to be careful."

"Then let's go with your gut."

He eyed the back door. "We could make a run for it, but…if it is the FBI, they need answers and we've done a lot of research. They won't take kindly to us ignoring them while we try to break this case. If we run, they'll track us, too."

"I agree," she said. "But if it's those goons, they might have us surrounded and we'll both get killed."

Another knock. "Craig, let us in. We need to talk to Alisha Braxton."

"Give me a minute," Nathan shouted through the door. He turned to Alisha. "Get your cell and put your cape and bonnet on and be ready to run. Look for the birdhouses."

"I'm not going without you."

"Alisha, don't argue with me. I'll have to hold them off."

She shook her head but went to the bench by the back door to grab the dark cloak her grandmother had loaned her. It wasn't regulation Amish since it had pockets but Granny had shoved it at her because it was warm.

Just to be sure, she gathered whatever she could into her briefcase and placed it behind the couch but kept their latest handwritten notes tucked along with her cell phone in the bib of her apron. When she reached down inside the case, her hand hit her pepper spray. She took it out and dropped it into the deep pocket of her cloak, thanking the Lord for that one secret compartment.

Another knock. And then the door rattled. Alisha's pulsed pounded against her temple while she tried to take her next breath.

Nathan put a finger to his lips and motioned for her to get behind him. "Remember, if you have to run, look for the birdhouses. They line the trail from the cabin to my folk's place."

Bobbing her head, she prayed she wouldn't have to go anywhere without him.

"I need to see some ID," Nathan called. "I'll open the door and you slip your badge through."

Alisha heard mumbling and shuffling. "I have my badge out."

Nathan kept the chain lock on the door and opened it just enough to see the badge. Alisha peeked at it from behind him.

It looked official enough but how could they be sure?

Before Nathan could confirm, the door flew open with a bang, ripping the chain lock away and knocking both of them to the floor. The breath went out of Alisha but she scooted up, ready to make a move if Nathan would go with her.

Then a shot and the back door swung open, a man with a rifle trained on them filling the cold space. She couldn't see his face in the muted lamplight, but she could tell he stood tall and bulky. The air hit Alisha's warm skin like a cold breath. No way out.

Nathan managed to hold onto his gun, his body a solid wall in front of where Alisha huddled on the floor. "Stay behind me, Alisha," he whispered. "But get ready to run."

"What about you?"

"Don't worry about me. I'll distract them."

Two men entered the house from the front and stood over them. Nathan held his gun toward the men at the door and then spoke to the one who'd just shot out the back lock. "That was rude."

"It's a little late for you to be whining," the first agent said as he flashed his badge again. "We've been looking for Miss Braxton for two days."

Nathan shook his head then sat up. "Breaking and entering is not a good idea. And holding that rifle on us only makes things worse."

One of the men closed the door behind him. The first one who'd flashed his badge said, "I'm Special Agent Mack Smith." Motioning behind him, he added, "This is Agent Scott Kemp and that fellow over there is Adam Baker. Why don't you relax and put down that gun, son."

Nathan checked the IDs they briefly held up but he didn't drop his weapon. "I guess you want to question my client. So I'll put down my weapon when you do the same."

The one named Mack nodded to the man holding the rifle. He lowered his gun. Nathan carefully placed his weapon on the floor.

"You could say that," Mack Smith replied, his gaze sliding over Alisha. "If it's not too much trouble we do need to question *your client*. I mean, this is a federal case and you're the only eyewitness, Miss Braxton. You don't need to run from the FBI."

"Who told you I was here?" Alisha asked, her tone firm and calm, while her eyes moved over the men. She had to find a way to get them out of this, but they were blocked in.

"We asked around," Mack Smith said with a slight smile.

Alisha had already figured out these people were not FBI, but her radar went up. Something was definitely off. They were all three dressed for the weather in heavy canvas jackets and jeans. But they didn't have the clean-cut look most FBI agents adhered to. The two backups were scruffy. One had a beard and from what she could see, the one standing at the back had long hair.

Alisha studied the two standing nearest and when her gaze moved to the other man—Adam Baker—she glanced at his haggard features and confirmed he had stringy long dark hair. Then she looked him in the eye.

The man stared back, a smug expression moving across his face, his eyes black and cold. Dead inside.

She gasped, causing Nathan to turn his head. That gave the intruders just enough time to make a move. The one holding the rifle rushed across the room and hit Nathan over the head with the butt of the weapon.

Alisha screamed as Nathan moaned and crumbled to the floor. Alisha scrambled to reach Nathan's gun, grabbed it up and shot at the one they'd called Scott Kemp. Her bullet hit his leg. He shouted in pain, his thigh gushing blood, and fell just inside the door.

"Help me," he called to his buddies.

"Leave both of them," Mack said to his partner, slanting his head toward Nathan and the bleeding man. He held the rifle over Alisha. "Drop the gun." Nodding to his buddy Adam, he said, "They can kill each other, for all I care. We came for the woman."

Nathan moaned again and tried to roll over toward Alisha so he could get the gun. The one she'd recognized came at her, dragging her away from Nathan. Alisha held up the gun, determined to shoot it but the man knocked it out of her hand, an ugly grin on his craggy face. Alisha screamed and kicked the gun away with her foot, praying Nathan would see it.

Her heart hammering, Alisha screamed again, kicking and fighting. The man with the long hair—the man she'd seen the night of the killings—had her by her cape collar, his stubby fingers digging into her skin. Leaning close, he whispered in her ear, his hot breath hitting her skin. "It's over now, lawyer-lady. No one will ever find you in these woods."

Alisha tried to scramble away, tried to grab her briefcase so she could use it as a weapon. But they lifted her like a rag doll and tossed her out the back door. The frigid air poured over her, freezing her to the spot for a split second. She turned, screaming for Nathan. A grungy hand slapped at her face and then covered her mouth.

"Scream again and we'll kill him in front of your eyes and then we'll kill you and your sweet gun-toting grandma, too."

Alisha turned back, panic in her throat, her lip bleeding, the cold wind chilling her to the bone. She had to do something. Nathan was injured and there was no way out. She'd wounded the other man but he could still get in a shot and kill Nathan.

Then she heard someone calling her name.

"Alisha!"

Nathan. He'd crawled to the door, his gun in his hand. He shot into the air but missed her captors.

One of them turned and shot back and she watched as Nathan slipped down the outside wall. And didn't move.

Nathan grimaced, the pain shooting through his shoulder excruciating. The bullet had gone through but he'd passed out for a few seconds and bled into the snow. He had to get to Alisha but he couldn't help her if he fell unconscious in the woods.

Dragging himself back inside, he pushed away the dizziness in his brain, a throbbing pain coursing through his temple like a roaring train. He managed to shut the door then he turned to where he'd seen Alisha shoot one of the intruders. The man was gone but he'd left a trail of blood out the other door.

Searching for a towel, Nathan dragged himself up and worked to stop the blood oozing out of his upper right shoulder. With a bit of effort and waves of dizziness, he hurriedly cleaned and bandaged it with supplies from the first aid kit he kept in the cabin. His head wound had stopped bleeding and the dizziness subsided once he settled down. But he couldn't stay settled.

Then he bundled up, checked the magazine on his gun and took some pain medicine for his headache. He'd tried to call for help but his phone's battery had gone dead. Too late for that. He had to track Alisha. Not sure how far ahead they were, he checked his supplies one last time and hurried to the back door. Stumbling, he hit his foot on Alisha's briefcase.

She'd said her life was inside that case. Right now, she didn't have it as her shield. He'd have to be her shield and pray that God was watching over them. His heart hammering an urgent beat, Nathan stashed her case under some clothes in the closet, put on a wool hat and his coat, then rushed out to begin the desperate race to find Alisha before it was too late.

TWELVE

She'd watched for the birdhouses.

Now Alisha saw them up ahead in the gray dusk. If she planned to make a run for it, now would be the time. Checking her pocket again, she held her fingers on the container of pepper spray. It had a stretch gripper band that she'd already slipped over her fingers. She used it mostly for jogging but now she was glad she'd kept an extra container in her briefcase. Being jostled here and there, she'd managed to unlock the safety. She was ready.

"Keep moving," Long Hair, or Ace as his friend called him, growled, hurling her forward. They all had nicknames. Mack the Knife, Ace, and Scooter. "Your man isn't coming to help you."

"He's not my man," she retorted. "But he'll find me. He's good at finding people."

"He's probably dead by now," the other one said. "Scooter wasn't hurt too bad."

She prayed Scooter had either left in a hurry or passed out cold.

Ace held her arm in a tight grip that was sure to leave bruises in the shape of his meaty fingers, while the other one kept watch behind them. They didn't speak much except to let her know that if she ran, she'd die and then they'd kill her grandmother.

Alisha had to go on faith. She would escape and she would find someone to help her and save her grandmother, too. This wasn't going to end in the cold woods. She'd do as Nathan had told her and run along the birdhouse path and find someone, anyone, to get back to him.

But as the two men pushed her toward the path she planned to take, they veered to the left instead of the right. Left was nothing but deep, snow-covered woods for miles. Right had a path and held hope. She had to act now or they'd have her back on the road and in a vehicle.

And then, she'd never have a chance to save anyone.

Ace yanked at her. "Keep up. We're almost there."

Alisha took a breath and said a little prayer for courage. Then she went limp.

"What's wrong?" Ace snarled, anger flashing in his eyes. "You'd better not be faking."

"I don't feel so good," she said, falling to her knees. I'm so tired and I need some water."

"We don't have water and you're walking," he said, trying to drag her up. "Someone wants to meet you."

Alisha was ready. Pulling her right hand out of her pocket, she sprayed him in the eyes and then turned toward the other man and did the same to him.

While they both screamed in agony, Alisha took off running with all her might. She had to get to the Schrock farm.

Nathan followed the path of the footsteps, thanking the snow for stopping long enough to give him a perfect trail. He was about twenty minutes behind and growing weaker by the minute, but he had to keep going. Three sets of prints until they got to the fork in the path. His pulse pressing against his temple, he blinked away pain and studied the trail. Three sets about five feet into the path to the left and then—

He stopped and knelt down, his mind whirling with the worst-case scenario. The snow was all smudged and gutted here, as if there had been a struggle.

Had Alisha gotten away?

Or had those two dragged her farther into the woods to the left?

He didn't know which path to take.

Lord, I need you. Guide me.

Nathan stumbled toward the other path, his breath fanning out in a cold fog in front of him. His body protested every step, his ears ringing with pain while his head throbbed. The bullet hole in his shoulder wasn't too happy, either.

But he kept trudging.

And found one set of footsteps digging through the deepening snow.

"Did you get away, Alisha?"

He looked around and realized he was on the birdhouse path. Squinting, he put one foot in front of the other and trudged ahead, not knowing if the prints belonged to her or not. But who else would be out here?

When he heard a rustling up ahead, Nathan dragged himself off the trail and hid in the snow-covered undergrowth behind a large pine. Something moved to the east. He could hear footfalls.

He watched, holding his breath, the Beretta Alisha had left behind tight against his fingers. He hoped she'd kept going.

The air shook with an echo of footfalls. A massive

shadow fell across the white snow, casting long in the waning moonlight.

Nathan braced for what might come.

The big stag strolled along the path, heading in the direction Nathan had just come. Breathing a sigh of relief, Nathan watched as the animal stopped and lifted his head, his nostrils flaring, his eyes watchful.

Then he looked in the direction of where Nathan was hiding. The deer didn't move and Nathan was afraid to move.

The big animal seemed to be standing guard, watching, waiting, listening. Then he turned around and took off, leaping back to the right.

Nathan decided he'd follow the stag.

Maybe the Lord had sent him another sign.

The stag left him behind, but Nathan saw a clear path now. The same smaller set of prints moved up the path, past the birdhouses he'd built and placed here, one at a time, from the time he'd moved into the cabin until now. He'd made a birdhouse to represent every celebration he'd missed with his family—birthdays and Easter, Christmas, summer, fall, winter and spring. A dozen or so, each unique and meaningful to him. He'd often walked this path, his creations bringing him joy and a sense of home. He enjoyed watching the birds make their nests there in the tiny houses and he'd watched their babies learning to fly away. He often wondered if anyone from his family had noticed the houses set along this remote path.

He'd never known that one day those little treasures, along with the stag that he'd befriended and obviously called this forest his domain, would take him back on the path toward home. Or back toward Alisha.

Please let her be safe. Let her be okay. Let her be alive.

He prayed silently and sometimes in soft whispered pleas. He would keep praying until he had Alisha in his arms again.

Alisha blinked and tried to focus. But the darkness seemed to close in around her with the same cloying strength as the men who'd tried to take her.

She'd gotten away and then she'd gotten lost. They'd both left earlier but then she'd heard them again, arguing about what to do, their voices getting closer. She kept running east but she'd gone off the open trail to stay hidden.

The two men had left abruptly due to a scare earlier, but now the darkness made it hard for her to see in the sloping hills surrounding Campton Creek. The cold chill that held her in ice, coupled with the shock coursing through her body, made her disoriented and tired. So tired.

Maybe she'd dreamed the whole thing. The two men screaming after she'd pepper-sprayed them, making sure she'd hit them in the eyes and face.

Ace had grabbed her, knocked her down and dragged her back.

"I'm going to end this here and now. I'm tired of chasing you around these aggravating hills and streams. They can't pay me enough for this kind of stuff."

She'd seen the rage in his dark, red-rimmed eyes. Evil permeated the air around him. He'd kill her without any qualms.

Then a swooping sound and something big and wild had leaped toward them and practically plowed into the man holding her. He'd been so taken by surprise and so terrified that he'd screamed and run away. After cursing at him, his friend had joined him.

The big deer with the massive antlers had scared off her captors. Alisha had managed to get up and run as fast as she could in the deep snow.

Except she'd veered off the path and now it was dark and the snow had started falling steadily again. Exhausted, she sat down near the trunk of a billowing oak tree.

"I'll just rest for a minute," she said into the night. "Just to catch my breath and find my way out of here."

Her last thoughts before a sweet sleep took over were of Nathan. *Please keep him safe, Lord.*

Nathan prayed all the prayers of his childhood, in both English and the Pennsylvania Dutch he'd grown up speaking, all the while searching with his tiny flashlight for any sign of Alisha. He should have found her an hour ago but the footprints he'd followed had taken a turn into the woods to the northeast and a new snow had covered them. He'd lost her trail.

He was lost and now he feared that Alisha was also.

He was also in pain. His arm and shoulder throbbed but he kept applying snowballs, placing a handful of the white slush over the sleeve of his jacket to cool down the wound and hopefully stop it from bleeding. His forehead had a knot on it that complained with each heartbeat.

But he kept trudging in the way the big deer had charged because with his mind so fuzzy, Nathan was running out of options. He'd follow his only ally in this forest.

A scant moonlight guided him deeper into the woods. When he heard a stream gurgling down the hillside, he watched and listened. He hadn't spotted Mack and the one named Adam, but Nathan knew how criminals operated. If Alisha had gone off into the woods, they'd either hidden to wait for an opportunity or, more likely, given up the chase.

Cowards, but he was glad for that. Their boss wouldn't be happy but Nathan didn't care about that right now. If he could find her before they did, Nathan would be able to hide her somewhere secluded and safe.

He made it to where the stream ran through the foothills and shined his flashlight around the woods, touching it on shifts and shadows. When he spotted fresh footprints in an opening leading down toward the water, he knew he was on the right track.

And that's when he saw her.

Alisha, lying curled up and asleep by a tree, snow covering her body without consideration or discrimination.

A freezing snow.

"Alisha?" he called, a catch in his voice, a rip in his heart. "Alisha?"

She didn't respond. Nathan slid down the rocky hillside, tumbling and tripping until he fell a few feet away from where she lay. Crawling and clawing his way to her, he lifted Alisha into his arms.

"Alisha?" She was cold, almost blue with cold. He rubbed his hands over her coat and then her face. She didn't have on a hat or gloves.

Feeling for her pulse, he let out a relieved breath when he felt a weak beat. Another hour or so and he might have lost her for good. Now they might have a chance.

Lifting her up, he held her in his arms and leaned back against the tree, the urge to sleep here with her so strong that he had to blink it away. His shoulder throbbed in protest, but he couldn't let her go. "We're going to be okay. We'll find shelter and you'll wake up warm and safe."

She didn't move or respond.

Nathan didn't know how he'd get her up the hillside, but he'd find a way. Reluctantly, he laid her back against the tree and took off his jacket to put over her. His long-sleeved shirt was torn and covered with blood. He didn't care.

Looking up, he pointed his light to the hillside and searched for a way up. Seeing some grooves and ledges up past the tree, he decided that would be the best way to go.

He shined the light up higher and saw something else.

The big stag standing there, his antlers spread out in perfect symmetry, his dark eyes on Nathan.

"Thank you," Nathan called on a hoarse whisper. "We're going to go home now and leave you to stand watch."

The stag lowered his head to the ground, snorted and then shook out his mantle in what could have been a parting gesture. Then he leaped away and pranced off into the woods.

Nathan found the strength he needed. Taking back his jacket, he tugged Alisha's still body up and into his arms and started the slow process of getting her up the hill and back to the path that would take them to a warm, safe place.

His parents' home.

His first attempt didn't work. His boot hit on a wet patch of rock and he slipped down, falling onto his backside, Alisha still in his arms.

"That didn't go so well," he said. With a grunt, he stood and rearranged her, one hand around her back and one holding her underneath her knees. "To be such a tiny woman, you sure are weighty."

But she was strong and buff. High-powered lawyers had to stay in shape.

"My *mamm* will make you the best soup and she'll have Christmas cookies in every cabinet. She'll get you in a warm bed and shoo me away while she fusses over you."

He hoped. He prayed.

Lord, please let them accept us. Please. I pray they won't turn us away.

Gritting his teeth, Nathan kept finding footholds, his mind on one step at a time. One step and then another step. Finally, he reached the top of the hill and worked his way across the woods and back toward the open trail. His flashlight, gripped loosely in his weak hand while he held onto Alisha, showed him the way. He saw hoof prints along the same path.

"Now you're just showing off, Old Stag."

But those hoof prints lead him to the path and then he turned east.

Toward home.

THIRTEEN

Nathan didn't think he could take one more step. He'd been walking for over an hour, Alisha in his arms. She was still asleep and that worried him. But he held her so tightly to his shoulder he could feel her heartbeat against his own.

At least she was warmer now, her warmth helping him to stay focused as he trudged through the hills and made it onto the old country lane that led up to the front door of his childhood home.

Heaving another grunt as he shifted Alisha in his arms, Nathan whispered in her ear. "We're here. That house right there is my parent's place. You'll be okay. I promise."

Stopping as the house came into view, Nathan's body surged with a homesick longing. How he'd missed his family. Why had he stayed away so long?

Memories reminded him of why he'd run like a coward and never looked back. He couldn't bear the burden of his family's grief, a grief that he felt so responsible for.

Alisha moaned in his arms, reminding him of the here and now. He didn't need to be standing here in uncertain fear.

So he started walking, wondering how he'd explain

this but hoping he wouldn't need to. He made it half-way up the drive and stopped again, fatigue dragging him down.

"I hope they're home." Realizing Alisha and he had been in the woods for most of the night, he said, "It's almost dawn, so they should be up anyway. Farm work, you know."

"Maybe this is a bad idea," Alisha said in a weak whisper. "They don't approve of me."

Looking down at her, Nathan couldn't help but smile. "You got any better ideas?"

"No." Her eyes closed again but at least she had woken up. That had to be a good sign.

Nathan said another prayer, thinking he'd caught up on his quota in one long, horrible night.

He was within yards of the houses when the front door swung open. Martha Schrock came running down the steps, her dark dress and black apron billowing out around her. "Nathan?"

Nathan nodded and stumbled closer. "Hi, Mamm. It's me."

Martha's face filled with concern. "What has happened?"

"I'll explain, but I need to get her inside and warm first."

Martha stopped as she got closer to them and saw the woman wearing a dark bonnet in his arms. "And who is this?"

Nathan glanced back at the road. "Mamm, I'll explain everything. May we come inside? She's been exposed to the cold all night."

His father stepped out onto the porch, a frown marring his face. His mother whirled to her husband. "Nathan has returned, Amos. He and this woman are in need."

For two heartbeats the morning went silent. Alisha moaned again and snuggled closer to Nathan. He kept glancing back as he inched her and his mother forward, afraid those men would be lurking about.

Finally, he said, "Daed, I need your help. May we please come inside?"

The plea in that question must have torn through his mother. Her eyes grew misty. She turned to her husband. "Amos?"

"*Alleweil*, Daed?" Right now.

Amos Schrock stared at them but didn't move.

"Amos?" His wife's plea sounded as heartbreaking as Nathan's had. "Our son needs our help."

Amos nodded. "*Ja.*"

Then he turned and went back inside the house.

Feeling dejected, Nathan moved forward. But to his surprise, his father came back out with two blankets and handed them to Martha. She nodded, unable to speak, and then hurried to cover both of them.

"*Kumm*, and let's get you both warmed up."

Martha shot her husband a sweet smile. "*Denki*, Amos."

Amos nodded and guided them up the steps. When they were inside, Nathan's parents turned to see the woman in his arms.

Martha gasped and Amos frowned.

Martha glanced over at Alisha, unable to speak as recognition spilled over her features. "Alisha?"

Alisha opened her eyes and focused. "Yes, Mrs. Schrock. It's me. And I'm so sorry to bother you."

Then she passed out again.

Nathan interjected, weariness and dizziness overtaking him. "We're in trouble, Mamm."

Martha gave Alisha another concerned stare, as if to say she'd already figured that out. Then she motioned to the downstairs bedroom on the back of the house. "*Druwwel*? What kind of trouble?"

Nathan felt as if he was shifting, his legs going weak. Following his folks, he said, "I... I need to lay her down."

His mother pulled back the quilt and fluffed the pillows. "Put her here."

He gently placed Alisha on the bed and tugged her out of her cloak while his mother held the blanket they placed over her. Alisha came awake, her eyes going wide.

"Where am I?"

"You're safe now," Nathan said, his voice hoarse as he covered her from her neck down, making sure she'd be warm. "Just as I promised."

He blinked, stumbled against the high-backed chair by the bed, his arms throbbing from carrying her for so long, his shoulder on fire. Pushing off the blanket, he tried to stay on his feet. And failed.

"Nathan, you're hurt!"

His mother's frantic shouts echoed all around him before he slumped over in the chair, unable to keep his eyes open any longer.

She woke to voices.

A soft voice. "The poor girl is exhausted. No wonder. She almost froze to death. And you with a hole in your shoulder."

A harsh voice. "You bring her here, to our home? You and your *Englisch* world? I had no choice but to help you this morning, but I won't have it. You can't stay here, Nathan."

A tired voice. "I told you, I have nowhere else to go right now. She needs to stay out of sight for a while."

Sitting up, Alisha glanced around the clean, plain bedroom, the sun shimmering through the windows. A beautiful bed with a colorful diamond-patterned quilt that would be worth hundreds of dollars hanging in a city store, along with a side table and a chair and a small wardrobe. Simple, stark and beautiful. A house full of love.

The sun shined high up in the sky, telling her it had to be mid-afternoon. She'd slept all day?

Her mind foggy, she remembered bits and pieces of conversations. Nathan talking softly in her ear out in the forest. His parents wrapping both of them with blankets, their voices filled with worry and surprise.

They'd taken her in. The parents that had not approved of her long ago had taken her into their home. Because they still loved their wayward son.

But she'd brought conflict and confusion back into this house when Nathan clearly needed to find redemption and peace. She saw clearly now. As clear as the glass vase holding a few pine boughs. A simple gesture to celebrate Christmas in a plain and quiet way.

"What do you plan? To shoot people dead in our yard?"

"Enough," Alisha said to herself in a mumbling whisper. "Enough." She had to get out of here, for Nathan's sake, if nothing else.

Pushing back the warm quilt, she got up to get dressed, a slight dizziness causing her to sit back on the bed. She ran her hands through her hair and padded her way across the old linoleum floor to use the indoor facilities she spotted in a small room across the hallway by the kitchen. After finding her now-clean clothes drying in what looked like a combination mud and laundry room, Alisha dressed and went into the living room to catch Nathan and his father in a stare-off, the large dining table between them. Nathan's arm was now tied with a white linen sling and a cloth bandage covered the wound on his shoulder. He also wore clean clothes. But he looked tired, dark circles underneath his eyes. Had he slept at all?

Taking a deep breath, Alisha said, "I'll leave."

They whirled to see her there. Amos turned an embarrassed red while Nathan fumed in frustration.

Martha rushed toward her. "Did you sleep well?"

"Yes, thank you." Alisha wasn't sure what to do or say. "I didn't realize how exhausted I was."

Nathan came around the table. "You need to eat."

"No," she said. "I need to leave. It's obvious I shouldn't be here."

Nathan shook his head. "No. It's not safe. I saw a truck roaming the roads this morning already. We need to stay hidden for a day or so." When she frowned, he added, "You're tired and recovering and my arm is still not in full working mode. We need to rest."

"She has a *gut* point," his father said, holding his own stare. "You shouldn't be here."

Martha touched Alisha's arm but gave her silent husband a firm stare. "Amos, I think they can stay a while. It is snowing and so cold and those people could still be around here somewhere. I made chicken and dumplings for supper. I'd like to share that with my son and Alisha. They are both wounded and need nourishment."

Amos grunted, the jagged wrinkle between his eyes deepening. "This is not our way, Martha."

"It is not my nature to turn away someone in need," his wife replied. "Especially when it is our son who has come to us injured and asking for our help."

Alisha watched the silent war between Nathan's parents. Amos Schrock caved to no one, except Martha Schrock. Nathan used to laugh about that, proud that his demure mother knew how to get her way when she wanted. Seemed this was one of those times.

"It's all right," Alisha said. "I can call a cab."

Nathan didn't argue with her but his eyes went dark. He looked weary but she was relieved that his shoulder was bandaged. She prayed his wound wouldn't get infected but his mother seemed adept at such things.

"You're not leaving," he finally said. "At least not without me."

Alisha realized his sacrifice. He'd come for her in the woods, wounded and hurting, and carried her all the way to this house. Instead of threatening to leave, she should be thanking him. She'd do that later when things weren't so tense.

Martha shook her head. "I am going to feed you both and let you rest. We will decide about what happens after that."

Amos nodded, silently and without any more arguments.

They'd been given a reprieve. One Alisha did not want or deserve. But Nathan needed this time with his parents, so she remained quiet.

Nathan watched as his father walked out of the room and then shifted his gaze toward Alisha. "How are you?"

"A little wobbly," she said, holding onto the wall.

"Come and sit at the table," he said, taking her arm. She didn't argue. The smell of strong coffee captured her attention. Spotting the coffeepot, she refused to be rude and beg for a cup.

Nathan read her mind. "Mamm, may I pour Alisha some coffee?"

"*Ja*," his mother said. "Where are my manners?"

Her tone was kind but hesitant. It had to be difficult, seeing her son again under such extreme circumstances.

"I'd so appreciate that," Alisha said. "I can't believe how long I slept."

"You were in a bad way," Martha said after she handed Nathan two cups of coffee. "You slept through Nathan's complaining about me cleaning his wound."

"It burned," he admitted with a smile. "But Mamm knows her way around an injured son since she has three."

"*Ja*, ain't so?" His mother chuckled and then offered Alisha a warm biscuit with a smear of apple preserves. "To tide you over until supper."

Waiting until she'd sat down at the long wooden table, Nathan took the coffee his mother offered and sat across from Alisha. "I got word to Carson about our intruders. He found out the officer in the deer stand in the woods was injured but managed to call it in. Two officers arrived at the cabin not long after I left but the snow became so heavy, they called it a night on doing a search."

Alisha remembered that thick, cold snow. Thankful for the warmth flowing around her now, she asked, "Are you okay?"

Nathan nodded. "I've been through worse." Then he went on with his report. "I gave Carson the names they used so based on their descriptions and the names, they'll run a check. Searched the woods as they backtracked toward the road and found one man. He's in a hospital nearby, under custody, but refusing to offer up any information."

Lowering her voice while his mother went about her chores, she whispered, "Obviously, they didn't find the other two."

"No. But they found a blood trail from the one in custody. That might give them DNA for evidence against him at least. And they think they spotted the dark pickup the men were driving."

Alisha let go of a shiver. "I don't feel comfortable here."

"And you'd be better off out there?"

Martha called to them. "Let her eat in peace, Nathan."

Alisha dropped things for now and nibbled on the biscuit. It was good but she couldn't seem to get much of it down.

Martha looked at her son. "Nathan, would you go and find your father? Supper will be ready soon."

Nathan hesitated and then did as his mother asked.

After he'd gone out the back door, a blast of cold air sneaking through before he shut it, Martha turned to Alisha and pointed to a stool. Then she brought her own cup of tea over.

"I think this is a good time for you and me to have a nice talk, Alisha Braxton."

Alisha didn't know whether to run back to the bedroom or just head out the front door and meet her fate.

Martha waited, a slight dare in her blue eyes.

"Of course, Mrs. Schrock," she said, taking the stool.

FOURTEEN

While he wondered how his *mamm* and Alisha were faring alone at the house, Nathan silently helped his father check on the animals and freshen their hay. The horses, milk cows and goats had mostly been fed their big meal early this morning, depending on their feeding schedules. His father had an internal alarm clock that had him up before the sun, checking on animals and going about the work of the farm. Unable to sleep earlier, Nathan had watched his *daed* out the window from his old room upstairs. He hadn't gone down then, afraid his father wouldn't want him to help.

But now, he'd gotten beyond his earlier hesitance. His *daed* might resent him being here and disapprove of all that Nathan had become, but he was home and Christmas was coming in a couple of days. Time to find the courage to face his father.

So here he was doing the chores that came back to him as easily as eating his mother's pancakes. And all the while, scanning the horizons and the edge of the woods for any lurkers or intruders. He'd not seen any trucks roaming the road but he had to wonder who could be lurking just beyond the hills and valleys.

But the land sat settled and quiet, as old and comfortable as the clothes he'd borrowed and wore now. No signs of anyone waiting to attack. He hoped things would stay quiet for a while.

Once Amos seemed satisfied with the animals, he moved on to the chicken coops to make sure the hens were warm and safe. The ornery rooster chased after Amos, but his father ignored the arrogant bird. Nathan followed, waiting for his silent *daed* to speak.

Amos moved on to the woodpile and grabbed an ax.

He offered it to Nathan, who, surprised but pleased, took it and watched as his father found another. Together, they began to chop wood to use to back up the propane tanks they kept to run appliances. His mother still loved her wood stove and used it during the worst of winter.

"Christmas Eve is tomorrow and then we have Christmas and visiting day after that," Amos said, pointing out the obvious. "You can stay through Christmas but I expect you to honor your faith by not bringing the *Englisch* violence into our home."

"I will do my best to keep this situation nonviolent."

"What if these men show up here, Nathan?"

"I'll lure them away from the house and keep everyone safe."

He hoped. He'd have to find his weapon and create a distraction. But Nathan decided he'd fight that battle when it came.

"How does the violent work you do honor the Lord?"

"My work isn't always like this," Nathan tried to explain. "I've helped a lot of people, mostly Amish, locate their kinfolk. I also help solve crimes by finding the truth."

Amos looked out over the fields. "Such as this one?"

"Yes, such as this one."

Following his father's example, he placed a round

log on the chopping block and then looked at his father.
"I never stopped honoring God. I just do it in a different way now."

The *Englisch* way," Amos said, hitting wood so hard
it easily split into kindling.

"Yes, different traditions but the same God."

"So you attend church regularly?"

He had Nathan on that one. "When I can."

"When you are not out there searching for evil people?"

"Or missing people." Nathan couldn't admit he hadn't
darkened a church door in a long time. "Yes, when I
can," he repeated.

"Your mother has missed you."

Chop, split. Chop, split.

"I've missed all of you, too." Nathan chopped a few
more logs and laid them in the wheel barrel. "How are
my brothers?"

"Gideon works at the Bawell Hat Shop which has expanded into a big retail business. Raesha Bawell married a man named Josiah Fisher a year ago. Josiah has
taken on some of the work at the shop so Raesha can
raise their children. They are raising his niece and Raesha is expecting her first baby this spring. Gideon loves
his work there. His wife Emma is also with child so she
and Raesha have bonded over motherhood."

"That's good news. He always did have a crush on
his Emma."

"*Ja*, and finally admitted it and asked for her hand
in marriage."

Nathan grinned. His father had spoken more than a
few words. He was sharing real news. "Maybe I can see
him during Christmas."

"They are coming the day after. Don't bring any harm on him."

The silence after that remark marred the conversation and caused Nathan to glance up again. A movement in the woods caught his eye. When a covey of quail flew out of the brush, he chalked it up to an animal moving past. But the hair on the back of his neck stood up anyway. Glad Alisha was safe inside, he watched for a moment longer but saw nothing.

Nathan tried again with his father, hoping to shake off his jitters. "And Thomas?"

Amos looked out over the fallow, snow-covered hills. "He is *gut*. He likes his life in Ohio. His wife's family *wilkumed* him with open arms. He loves her two children like his own."

"I'm glad they are both okay," Nathan said, meaning it. "I have visited Thomas a time or two. Beautiful community."

Winded and spent, Amos slapped his ax against the chopping block and turned to face Nathan. "How are you, son?"

Nathan's eyes pricked with a wet sheen, whether from the cold air or the kindness in his father's quiet question.

"I've had better times, Daed. I can't let anything happen to Alisha."

Amos rubbed a hand down his beard. "So you still to this day have feelings for this woman?"

"I'll always have feelings for her," Nathan admitted. "We might have been wrong for each other but… I can't forget her. And when she needed me, I had to go to her."

"So she *did* get you involved in this?"

Nathan looked for the condemnation in his father's stormy eyes, but was surprised and relieved to find none. "She witnessed a horrible murder and then they came after her to silence what she saw. Tried to run her off the road."

Amos nodded. "We heard two officers were in a bad accident near Green Mountain. Does that have something to do with her?"

"They were following her to make sure she got here safely."

"And someone caused their accident?"

"Yes." Nathan stared at the house, the cold settling over him as the wind picked up. "She witnessed that, too. She called me out of desperation, Daed. I couldn't say no."

Amos dusted his hands and turned toward the barn. His frown didn't show much but his eyes had softened. "That must have been a terrible burden for her to bear. I can see why she'd call someone she trusts."

Floored, Nathan could only nod. "I suppose so."

Did Alisha trust him? She'd come here under duress and because she was terrified. But he knew she could bolt and try to outrun these people on her own to protect his family and hers.

Once they reached the big double doors, Amos glanced around. "I'm sorry I was harsh earlier but seeing you at our door was both a joy and a shock. Your *mamm* is right, though. I can't turn away a family member in need. What is your plan?"

"I'm making that up as I go," Nathan admitted, accepting his father's apology as a victory. "If I can keep her hidden until we figure out who's coming after us, then we can put them away and she'll be able to testify in a court of law as to what she saw that night. I can't believe she managed to get here safely after they came after her so fast."

"But she brought harm on her *grossmammi* and Mrs. Campton."

"She needed a safe haven. They didn't question that. We have security at the Campton Center day and night and officers on patrol there. We also put out the word that we were headed back to Reading, but unfortunately, that didn't fool them."

"Reading?"

"She works for a law firm there that also has offices in Philadelphia."

"Where do you live?"

Nathan thought about his secluded little cabin. As far as he knew, his family wasn't aware it belonged to him. "I travel a lot and stay in rented apartments or hotels."

"That is no way to live."

"It's the only way I know."

Amos waited for him to enter the barn. "But you are home now, son. And for that, I am thankful."

Nathan let out a breath he'd been holding for over a decade. "Does that mean I'm forgiven for leaving?"

"There is nothing to forgive. God will see us through."

"But you were so angry—"

Amos held up a hand. "I was angry about a lot of things but I've had many days and nights to think about my actions since then. That was a bad time for all of us, but we accept it as God's will. I should not have taken out my anger on you."

Nathan wanted to ask his father about Hannah. Did he ever wonder why this terrible thing had to happen to one so innocent? Did he believe that what happened to her was God's will? But he held off on that. He wouldn't upset his father after such an honest talk. He'd do what his father had suggested. He'd accept things for now because he had to keep Alisha alive so they could get these people put away for a long time.

After that, Nathan would become that nomad again, wandering and always on the move. But he didn't think he'd ever be able to chase his pain away.

Alisha looked into Martha Schrock's eyes and wished she could figure out what Nathan's mother truly thought about her. "What would you like to discuss?" she asked, cutting to the chase.

"You've been through a terrible ordeal," Martha said, shaking her head. "To witness something so horrible. What a shock for you."

Surprised at the compassion in Martha's blue eyes, Alisha bobbed her head. "It happened so quickly and then I had to go into hiding when they came after me. But I was concerned for my grandmother and Miss Judy. So we went on the run again and then they came again. I think the shock caught up with me."

"More than shock," Martha replied as she got up to stir the good-smelling soup. "You almost froze to death. Nathan was right to bring you here."

"But now, we've put you in danger—if those men find us."

"I'm not worried about that," Martha replied, her hand touching Alisha's arm. "I am more concerned about my son."

"You're worried about Nathan?"

"*Ja.*" Martha moved her hand away but her smile was brief and soft. "He's been through some terrible things, too. I know he left because he blamed himself for our little Hannah's disappearance and…death. He and his father said things in anger that night that they both need to ask forgiveness for."

Thinking about what Nathan had also said to her, Alisha lowered her head. They were way past that now. "He wants to do that, I think. He told me he had unfinished business here with both of you."

"And yet, he brought *you* here."

"Do you resent that?"

"It's not my place to resent anything," Martha replied. "What I'm trying to say, what you need to see, is that he brought you here to help with that unfinished business. He wants to resolve things with us but he also wants to resolve things with you."

"He's trying to save my life. That's all," Alisha said, not wanting Nathan's mother to misunderstand. "Once I'm safe, Nathan will take off again."

Compassion lightened Martha's eyes. "Is that what my son does, takes off?"

Alisha wanted to be honest and Nathan's mom had a way of bringing out the honesty in people. "He's been running for over a decade now. He thinks he'll find all of the lost people in the world."

"He might," Martha said, her whisper so low Alisha barely heard it. "But then, he might not. Sometimes, they are found but…they are in the hands of God."

Wanting to bring Martha some comfort, Alisha said, "But sometimes Nathan finds them alive and reunites them with the people they love. That's important to him. It's his calling."

"So his calling keeps him from coming home to us?"

"No, his guilt takes care of that. He left all of us behind when he left Campton Creek."

"You still care for my son?"

Alisha wasn't ready to answer that. But she did nod. Then she said, "I'll always care for Nathan."

Now more than ever.

"I had to walk away because he couldn't stay," she admitted. "He couldn't stay with me and he couldn't come home. He's become a wanderer, a nomad without a permanent home. He can't move past what happened that night."

"But God sometimes moves those who can't find their own way," Martha said, tears misting in her eyes. "Nathan left us because of you and because of Hannah. Now, he has come home to us—for you and I think to find some peace with his sister's death. So despite what brought you both here, I pray he can let go of the pain and guilt of her death and just rest. Saving you from harm might actually bring my son his salvation."

FIFTEEN

The next afternoon, Nathan and Alisha sat at the dining table wearing more borrowed Amish clothes. Earlier that morning, Alisha had helped his mother with the washing machine, which ran with a paddle powered by hand. Martha had shown her how to clean their clothes with lye soap. They worked together in the small side room off the kitchen, where Alisha and Nathan had taken turns freshening up.

This room was used for laundry, bathing and as a mudroom—clothes hanging on a stringed line to dry over a small propane heater along with coats, boots and work shoes lined up along the wall underneath the clothing pegs. All neat and tidy and simple but with efficient indoor plumbing discreetly hidden behind another small enclosure. For which Alisha was eternally grateful.

While they'd worked, Martha had talked about Nathan growing up here with his younger brothers. She even mentioned Hannah a couple of times.

"*Gut kinder*, but rambunctious," Martha said, shaking her head. "But Nathan always did have a curiosity about life outside of Campton Creek. Wanderlust, I think. I prayed he'd come home after his *rumspringa*, but God had other plans for my son."

Alisha wanted to tell his mother she was so sorry that she'd interfered with those plans. He might have returned home if she hadn't become his forbidden sweetheart.

But before she could voice that, Martha turned to her and gave her a hesitant smile. "It wasn't his fault, you understand. And it wasn't your fault, either. You both left because of a terrible thing. I think God has used this current horrible tragedy to bring you both home."

Logic told Alisha she'd been in the wrong place at the wrong time when she'd pulled into that little Christmas market. That two people possibly involved with criminals had lost their lives and she happened to be the only person around to witness that. But here, in the quiet of this kitchen, another kind of logic took over. Had she been exactly where she should have been the other night?

Martha's eyes met hers. "You don't seem so sure about what I've said."

"I want to be sure," Alisha admitted, "but if God wants to bring us together, why does it have to be in such a violent way? With evil men murdering people, chasing us and threatening everyone we love?"

"Hmm, seems that happened in the Bible a few times, ain't so?" Martha let that observation hang in the air and then went back to her work, her deft hand holding Nathan's shirt against a scrub board.

"Good point." Alisha hung the dress she'd worn yesterday on the line and watched to make sure it wouldn't drip everywhere.

"Time will show us why, Alisha," Martha replied, her tone firm and calm. She carefully helped to hang the rest of their wet clothes on the taut line stretched across the mudroom. "But I believe that sometimes, we have to walk through the fire to find the calm we seek. Think about it. If you both survive this, you can survive anything, and your feelings will be stronger than ever. If that is *Gott*'s will."

"And what if someone else loses their life?"

"God's will always stands—and we must accept that no matter the pain."

Now, sitting here wearing a clean dress and apron, her hair pulled back in a ponytail and covered with a white *kapp*, Alisha marveled at how Nathan's parents had allowed them to stay. She felt secure inside these sturdy walls, cocooned by the snow outside. Their forgiveness now was in sharp contrast to what she remembered that awful summer way back. This home was roomy and simple, but full of God's grace. Why had it taken so long for Nathan to come back? Did time heal all wounds?

He might not have returned, if not for you.

Martha had been convinced of that. Alisha had to consider being here a blessing at least. No matter the circumstances, Nathan was back in the house he'd loved. She hoped that would bring him a time of healing. She didn't expect he'd return to the Amish, but if he could still visit with his family and be a part of their lives, it could all be worth it.

Alisha looked around, marveling at the simplistic beauty of the place. "It's Christmas Eve," she blurted, her gaze lifting toward Nathan. "I'd almost forgotten."

"Yes, it is." He gave her a smile. "We get to spend it here together."

His gentle words made her blush but she couldn't give in to all these erratic impulses she'd been holding so close. So she glanced around the room instead, searching for signs of the holiday.

The kitchen was sparse and neat, with a huge table that had to have been handmade years ago, along with matching high-backed chairs. A deep farmhouse sink held a pump for drawing water and a refrigerator that ran on propane sat full of prepared dishes for tomorrow. Alisha had offered to sweep the floor after dinner but Martha had shooed her away.

"I do that every morning to start the day fresh. You can do it tomorrow morning if you wish."

The home held bits of Christmas, but no tree or lights. Christmas cards from family and friends, most of them handmade, lined the wooden ridge of a big, practical sideboard across from the table. It held three freshly baked pies—pecan, sweet potato and apple—and two different cakes—a coconut layer cake and a pound cake that had been made from exactly a pound of each ingredient. Tomorrow, they would have a big meal of baked turkey, mashed potatoes, vegetable casseroles and all sorts of other side dishes.

"After devotionals and exchanging simple presents, we'll share the meal," Nathan had told her earlier. "If Christmas had been one day earlier, we'd have gone to church."

Alisha longed to see her grandmother, but today they were trying to map out their next move. "I should be there with Granny and Mrs. Campton," she whispered to Nathan. "I've waited all year to spend the holidays with them. It was the only gift my grandmother wanted." Shrugging, she added, "It's the only gift I want this year, too."

He stared over at her, both of them mindful of his mother puttering in the kitchen and his father sitting in his rocker reading an Amish newspaper. Alisha could tell being here had helped Nathan so much. She didn't want to mess with that.

"I'm sorry," he said, his hand touching hers in a brief

brush. "If I could make this all go away, that would be my gift to you."

"Your parents have been more than kind to me," she said, "so I don't mean to sound ungrateful. I just wish—"

"We both have our wishes," he said, his eyes going a dark blue that reminded her of a deep lake. "I'm going to get you back to your grandmother soon."

Since phone service was sketchy, and because they wanted to honor the rules of the house, they didn't use their phones to work. Their laptops were still at the cabin, she hoped. She missed her big briefcase with the shoulder straps. Her shield, her work companion. Nothing to be done about that now, though. Instead, they put together on paper a timeline of events based on the research they'd done already.

"The doctor had some major debts to pay," Nathan whispered. "The cars, the homes and too many charge cards. All a facade."

"That is a great motive to start selling opioids illegally," Alisha replied. "And to get in over your head with some nasty people. But the money had to be enticing."

"Yes, from what we've pieced together, I think he owed them money or drugs maybe, and when he couldn't pay up, they decided to off him and his wife."

Alisha stared at the timeline. "But that won't get these people their money back."

"No, but they could easily find a way to break into his offshore accounts if there's any money left in them."

Jotting a note to find out about those possible accounts, she asked, "But how do we nail Deke Garrison for this? The man is like a ghost. Nowhere to be found."

"He's hiding," Nathan said. "The hit was completed but you saw the whole thing. He'll kill his own men because they keep messing up. You got away over and over."

"Thanks to you," she said, her words low.

Nathan didn't respond with words, but his expression softened and shifted and for a brief moment, he looked like the boy she remembered.

Confused and too aware of him, she read over the names of the men, thinking about their clothes and faces. "I hope we get a hit on one of these men. They're relentless."

"The one they're guarding in the hospital should be easy to identify, even the name Scott Kemp has to be an alias. They've got his prints so that might get a definite hit. Since we can't get online here, I hope we hear soon."

Nathan leaned close. "After Christmas, I think we should go back to our plan and head into Philly. We can meet with the real FBI there. We'll have to be careful and we'll have to stay in disguise."

She glanced at his mother, wondering if she could hear them. "This is a federal case and we need all three of these men in custody. If I can identify one or more of them, I'll become a federal witness. I can't withhold what's been happening here any longer."

"Okay, so we plan to do this as our next step. But after Christmas. My folks will go visiting the day after tomorrow and they could have lots of visitors, including my brothers, the next day. We'll stay here after they leave and then we'll find a way to get to Philly."

"Okay, but I'd like someone from my firm there to represent me and guide me through the interrogations."

"Good idea."

It sounded like the best solution. Her firm could put law clerks on this and hire people to help protect her.

She couldn't stay here indefinitely and keep putting both of their families in danger.

"I'll call my boss first thing day after tomorrow," she said. "Let him know I do need his help." Mitchell Henderson would meet them in Philadelphia if necessary. Having someone she trusted to represent her would be wise.

"Are you two finished plotting over there?" Martha asked, her expression neutral. "I need help with a few things."

"Yes, Mamm," Nathan said. "I hope we didn't disturb you."

"You did not," his mother replied. "But this subject matter is terribly disturbing. I want you both safe."

Nathan got up to help his mother put away some food and baking dishes. "We'll let this go until after Christmas," he said, giving his mother a reassuring smile.

Martha touched a hand to his jaw. "I think that is a *gut* plan, Nathan. Tomorrow we celebrate not only the birth of our Lord Jesus, but we also celebrate the return of our oldest son." Then she added, "If you can't stay for Second Christmas, I understand."

Alisha couldn't help but hear. Second Christmas was always the day after Christmas where more casual visits took place, but still with lots of food and festivities. A visiting day, but the best time for them to leave since the roads would be bustling with Amish buggies.

After they'd helped Martha move the table to add more chairs in case they had visitors tomorrow, Nathan turned to Alisha. "I'm going to try and reach Carson and bring him up to speed. I'll be right outside."

"Okay. Be careful."

"I'll hide in the corner of the porch where the house takes an L-shape."

She smiled. "Watch out for Santa."

Watching him go, she let her heart do that little jumpy thing it seemed to want to do whenever he was near. She'd tempered her feelings for Nathan a long time ago, but even in the midst of fear and danger, he still made her heart beat too fast. He was her protector, her friend, someone she'd fallen in love with years ago and someone she'd tried to put out of her mind since. She'd never dreamed he'd come back into her life in such a big way.

She'd never dreamed anything like this could happen to her. Up until now, she'd been self-involved and focused on her work, lonely at times, but content and fulfilled.

She now appreciated all of that and more.

"*Kumm* and sit with us for a while," Martha said. "I have a few books and devotionals by my chair if you'd like to read a bit."

"Thank you." Alisha sat down across from them. "And thank you for everything."

Amos looked up at her but didn't speak. Martha nodded and glanced toward the door. "I am thankful you are both alive and well and here with us."

Alisha lifted one of the books off the table. A midwife story. That made her think about Nathan and marriage and children and…things she shouldn't be considering. Pretending to read the book, she instead held a vision of Nathan holding a child in his arms. He'd make a good father.

When Nathan came through the door, she exhaled the breath she'd been holding. Would she ever feel truly comfortable around his family? His folks, obviously feeling the same way, said good-night and went upstairs to bed, leaving them alone.

"Want to sit by the stove?" he asked, motioning her over to where the wood stove still held some heat.

Alisha didn't know why all of a sudden she felt shy around him. They'd been together for days. But it was too quiet here, too silent to hide the awareness that seemed to be simmering right below the surface of their fatigue and apprehension.

She sat in the cushioned rocking chair his mother had vacated, the scent of the locally made cinnamon candle sitting on a shelf still lingering in the air. "Did you talk to Carson?"

He hesitated and then nodded. "Yes. First he told me that my truck is being watched 24/7, according to his sources in Reading. Same dark SUV-type vehicle's circling the hotel parking lot."

"They've probably harassed everyone at the hotel to find out if you're there or not."

"Right. But that means they don't know where we are for sure. But they've managed to slip away before anyone can track them, so that's a problem."

"So we keep moving."

"Yes. Carson offered to escort us to the city but in an unmarked car. So we'll continue to dress Amish and take him up on that offer. That won't be so unusual this time of year with people visiting each other."

"If I show up dressed as an Amish woman, my boss will faint dead away," she said with a giggle as she stared down at the burgundy dress and white apron she was wearing. In spite of the seriousness of this situation, she had to laugh at that scene.

"I would think so, although you look pretty pretending to be an Amish woman." His eyes held hers for a brief moment and then he quickly gazed at the old potbellied stove. "We can't go back to your place in Reading. They're probably watching it."

"And they've probably already been inside," she replied, her heart skipping at that thought. She'd have to move. She didn't want to go back there at all now.

"So I'll rent us two rooms in a place I use in the city."

"That's fine."

Lifting an eyebrow, he said, "You don't sound so sure."

"It's just I never thought I'd be having this kind of conversation with you."

Nathan's gaze washed over her again and she saw it there in his eyes—the same longing that poured through her heart each time she looked at him. "No," he said, leaning close, "I always thought one day we'd go on our honeymoon and share a room, as man and wife."

Shocked at those words, Alisha looked down at her lap. "This sure isn't a honeymoon, is it?"

"No," he said. Then he reached across the side table and took her hand in his. "But a double murder and scary hit men aside, I wouldn't want to be anywhere else tonight."

Alisha took his hand and savored the warmth of his fingers curling over hers. "Merry Christmas, Nathan."

"Merry Christmas, Alisha."

He walked her to the door of her room but when he heard a rustling outside, he tugged her close. "Go upstairs."

Alisha watched from the landing as he went to a side window and stared out into the dark night. Hearing another noise, he motioned to her. "Go and get my gun from my room."

She hurried barefoot into his room, hoping she wouldn't disturb his parents. Since their door was shut and the small room he'd taken was down the hallway from theirs, she made it to his room and grabbed the weapon he'd put in the bottom of a small armoire when they'd first arrived.

Then she moved silently back down the stairs to find him roaming from window to window.

"Is someone out there?"

He nodded, waiting, a finger to her lips. "Go to your room but stay by the door."

Alisha didn't argue. She had to stay quiet. If his folks woke up, they could get caught in the crossfire.

Nathan came away from the window and called to her through the partially cracked door. "Listen to me. I'm going to go and check the barn. If I'm not back in five minutes, wake my *daed*, all right?"

She nodded, anxiety making her breath come too shallow. "Where does your father keep his hunting rifles?"

"You don't need to worry about that."

"Nathan, I know how to shoot a gun."

He shook his head. "He keeps them in the barn, locked in a cabinet. We can't get to them, so just stay in your room."

Alisha watched as he carefully opened the back door down the hall past the mudroom. She couldn't stay still so she went to her room and peeked between the modesty curtains, the moonlight shining brilliantly against the whiteout.

Nathan hurried in a hunched run toward the barn.

Then she saw a lone shadow moving around the west corner of the looming structure.

Grabbing a shawl she'd left on the bed, she hurried around to the back door. She had to warn Nathan.

SIXTEEN

She'd made it to a mushrooming old oak tree when she heard what sounded like a grunt, followed by an animal's whinny. After that, she heard muttered voices. Then she saw that same shadowy figure running toward the woods. Nathan came around the barn, watching as the man took off in a fast getaway and dived over the corral fence.

Nathan stood watching and then turned back toward the house. When he got close, she called softly. "Nathan?"

Surprised, he whirled and stomped toward where she stood hidden behind the massive tree trunk. "Why do you always insist on leaving your post?"

"Why do you always try to be a hero?" she retorted. "You could have been killed."

He took her in his arms and held her close, the tree blocking them from the house and the woods. "The same with you."

Alisha held him tight, feeling his heartbeat moving with hers. "Did you get a look at him?"

"Not a good one. But I warned him I had a pistol trained on him and I would shoot to kill. Then while he was pondering that, one of the old male goats gave him a run for his money. I'm surprised the noise didn't wake my parents."

"I heard a few grunts," she said, relief washing over her. "Do you think he's gone?"

"For now. He'd be an idiot to come back tonight."

Alisha looked up and saw Nathan gazing down at her, his eyes a deep blue in the shimmer from the moonlight. "We can't keep doing this," she said. "Because they won't give up."

"I know." He studied her as if he were trying to memorize her face and then reached a hand up, digging his fingers in her hair. "I know." Then he leaned down and touched his lips to hers. "I won't give up, either, Alisha."

His touch caused Alisha to pull him close and kiss him back. This wasn't like the adolescent kisses she remembered from the past. This was a grown man holding her in his arms, his lips conveying what he couldn't say and telling her they'd lived a million lifetimes since he'd last held her this way.

But the moment ended too soon. He pulled back to stare down at her again, a deep burning agony covering his face. "It's cold. We should get inside."

Alisha couldn't speak. He put his hand against her backbone and guided her toward the back door. They moved inside without making any noise, the house warm and quiet and still, as if holding its breath in the same way she was holding hers.

Nathan once again tugged her toward the door to her room. Then he shoved his pistol into her hand. "Keep that close. I'm sleeping in the living room tonight."

With that, he was gone, pulling her door shut before she could respond.

Alisha doubted either of them would get any sleep. They still had a lot between them—bad people wanting her dead, his family having to deal with all of this and the feelings they were both trying so hard to fight.

How would she ever make it through any of this? But how would she have made it this far without his help?

After she'd put on the billowy nightgown Martha had given her, Alisha lay in bed and said her prayers, the memory of that midnight kiss staying with her.

We need mercy, Lord. We need guidance. We need You. I've drifted away from my faith. I got caught up in work and loneliness and life. But I know You are there, always. I need You as my shield now. Nathan needs you. He's been carrying this horrible burden for a long time and he's forgotten how to love. Maybe we can show him that's still possible.

After she'd prayed, she closed her eyes and thought of how she'd felt when he'd held her and kissed her. She'd felt at home and at peace. If only she could feel that way forever.

The next morning, Alisha got up early to help Martha in the kitchen. After she'd dressed and made sure she looked as Amish as she could by wearing her hair pinned up underneath a white *kapp*, she checked her apron and dress and decided her own black boots didn't look too out of place since the heels weren't very high. Nathan had suggested they dress to blend in. Although his parents didn't expect any visitors until tomorrow, they had to take every measure to look the part. Especially after what had happened last night.

She wondered how exactly Nathan had slept, but figured he'd found a quilt and pillow and curled up by the stove. She also wondered if his parents had found him that way and asked for an explanation. She only knew something had changed between them there underneath that sheltering oak tree.

They'd both let down their guard. That could be so

good or it could turn out to be the worst thing for both of them. She had to talk to him and make sure he understood this could never work.

But when she walked into the living room, she didn't see Nathan or his father. Or Martha either.

A sense of panic overcame her. Where was everyone? She checked the side room and didn't find any of them. Then she went to the back door and searched the yard before looking out toward the fields and barn.

When she spotted Nathan coming out of the barn with his father, her relief was so great she closed her eyes and fell against the wall to gulp in deep breaths.

"Alisha, are you not well?"

Alisha looked up to find Martha standing in the kitchen, holding a basket of wrapped gifts.

"Oh, I'm sorry," Alisha said. "I couldn't find any of you and I got worried."

Understanding flowed through Martha's eyes. "I went into my chest upstairs to bring out our gifts," Martha explained. "I had to wait until the men were out of the house. Nathan was already up and out tending the livestock when we came down."

So that explained that. He'd probably gone out to the barn to search for any signs of that intruder.

"I can help you put the gifts out," Alisha said, her heart still racing. "Silly me. I'm not usually so jumpy."

"Understandable." Martha gave her a head-to-toe check, however. "You look very pretty this morning."

"Thank you," Alisha said. "Do you want me to take that?"

"We'll leave these things in the basket," Martha said, taking the beautiful woven basket over to the chairs. Placing it by the woodstove, she said, "When they return, we'll get started. But you can help me with breakfast."

"I'll be happy to."

When Martha started fluffing pillows, Alisha relaxed a little. But something about Martha's busy work shouted that the other woman, usually so serene, had something on her mind today.

Holiday stress? Or had Nathan told his parents about the intruder who'd been snooping around?

Alisha took another deep breath even as she sensed something was off. What were they all hiding from her?

Nathan and his dad waited outside the barn, Nathan to watch for any more interlopers, and his father to make sure their big surprise actually took place.

"They should be here by now," Amos said. "Are you sure your friend will be able to get them here?"

"Yes. I told him to come early," he replied, rubbing his hands together. "But those two have a mind of their own and they only move at one speed."

"Slow?" Amos laughed. "They are your elders so be mindful."

"Oh, I'm mindful," Nathan said. "They can hold their own."

Amos stood silent for a moment, one old boot caught against the fence railing. "Did you and Alisha take a moonlight stroll last night?"

Nathan tried to form an answer and decided to go with the truth. "We did. I heard a noise so I wanted to check the animals. She asked to come with me."

His father gave him a slanted glance. "I thought I heard voices. Your *mudder* said I was dreaming."

"We didn't stay out here long," Nathan replied, memories of their shared kiss warming his skin. "It was chilly."

Amos looked into his eyes. "Are you sure everything is all right?"

"Today, everything is perfect," Nathan replied, praying it so. "Or at least it will be when they get here."

He wondered if his father knew more but decided he'd explain later. After kissing Alisha, Nathan felt in over his head with trying to protect everyone and deal with his growing feelings again. He'd locked away those feelings forever, or so he'd thought. Getting all tangled up in these aching emotions did no good right now. He hoped Alisha would understand that.

Amos watched the road. "There, son. They are here."

Nathan's heart filled with joy. He couldn't wait to see Alisha's face. Would she like his Christmas surprise?

"Let us get to it then," his *daed* said with a soft smile. "Merry Christmas, Nathan."

"Merry Christmas, Daed."

They hurried to the house and had just entered the back door when they heard the buggy coming up the drive.

Martha turned and winked at him. "We have some very early guests arriving."

Nathan looked at Alisha and saw the apprehension in her eyes.

"Should we hide, Nathan?" she asked.

The fear in her voice flooded him. Who was he kidding? He'd walk through fire to protect her and hold her in his arms again. "I think we're safe."

Amos waved his hand in the air. "No hiding. These are *wilkum* guests."

Alisha's frown went from fearful to curious. Moving to the front of the living room, she peered out the window. "That's Josiah Fisher. Is he bringing his family to visit?"

"*Neh*," Martha said, holding a hand to her lips. "He is doing a favor for a friend."

Nathan couldn't hide his grin. "You'll see."

He moved to stand by her, so he could watch her face

while she watched the buggy. Alisha shot him one of the questioning glances he remembered before…before they'd become close again.

"Just relax," he whispered. "It's Christmas. Nothing bad can happen to us today." He'd make sure of that.

Then he motioned to the buggy.

Alisha followed Nathan's gaze and waited. What was he up to now? Did he plan to whisk her away and put Josiah in danger, too? She knew they were close since Nathan had helped Josiah find his missing sister Josie. Now the young woman lived with Josiah and Raesha and Raesha's former mother-in-law Naomi. She'd helped them with the same case, which had involved an abandoned baby that they were now raising. A happy ending.

But why involve Josiah in *this*?

Josiah waved to them and then went to the back of the buggy and untied what looked like a folded wheelchair. Then Nathan went out to carefully help the two Amish women out of the enclosed buggy, a slow process since they both appeared to be elderly. Unable to see who they might be since they were covered from head to toe in bonnets, shawls and cloaks, Alisha waited patiently.

After all, this wasn't her house. She couldn't make demands or run and hide. The others seemed so excited, she figured these two must be matriarchs of some sort.

After Josiah had one of the women in her wheelchair, he turned and nodded, a smile crossing his handsome face. Then the two women smiled.

"Let's go and greet them," Martha said, moving toward the door.

Nathan came hurrying back and took Alisha by the hand.

She watched as the two women looked toward the

house and then she saw their familiar faces. Gasping, she glanced at Nathan as he hauled her to the open front door. "Is that…my grandmother and Mrs. Campton?"

He bobbed his head. "It is. My Christmas gift to you."

"Nathan." She couldn't speak. Her eyes pricked with moisture. "Nathan."

His eyes grew misty. "Just for today, we'll pretend that everything is okay."

Amazed and touched, Alisha reached up and kissed him on his jaw. "Thank you."

Then she took off down the steps to hug her grandmother tight.

The next few minutes were a blur of hugs and happiness and both her grandmother and Mrs. C talking at once.

"We planned the whole thing—with Nathan's help, of course. And that sweet Carson. He is a true lawman—a hero. He's kept us up-to-date and coordinated things with our police department and so our place has been surrounded with guards."

"We decided we'd have fun with it and dress up in disguises in case anyone was watching. But we've been fine at our house. Those mean men know you're no longer there and that we have those dedicated guards always checking on us."

"And Josiah was so kind to leave his family to bring us here. He'll get extra cookies for his efforts, of course."

"They are staying for dinner," Martha explained after Josiah had said his goodbyes, a container of snickerdoodles on the buggy seat next to him. "And we will exchange gifts later."

"I don't have any gifts to give," Alisha said, her heart filling with love for their bravery in sneaking out to come here.

"Being here with you today is the best gift," Granny

said, her eyes welling up with tears. "We have prayed for both of you and when Carson let us know you were here, we were so relieved. We understand Nathan was injured and you ran away into the woods."

Alisha nodded as they all gathered in chairs by the warm stove. Martha and Nathan stayed in the kitchen preparing coffee and bacon along with homemade cinnamon rolls to tide them over until the big meal. She glanced up at Nathan and thought seeing his smile was the best gift she could ask for. He'd risked a lot, bringing these two women here to share Christmas with her. She'd never forget that.

"I did get away from the cabin," she said, taking a deep breath, the horror of that night still with her. She didn't go into too much detail. "After they shot Nathan, I was afraid they'd kill me, too. I had some pepper spray in my pocket and I used it. Then a big stag we'd seen earlier came charging through the woods and scared them away."

Nathan put down the dessert plates he'd taken down out of the cabinet and held his free hand against the sling his mother had changed out earlier. "Alisha, you saw the deer again?"

"Yes. I didn't think to tell you. He came along the path and almost rammed one of those men holding me."

"I saw the stag later too," he said. "In fact, spotting him helped me to find you." He shrugged. "Almost as if he led me to you."

Mrs. Campton, her bonnet still on, clapped her hands and smiled. "God's creatures can sense fear and danger, even evil, I believe. You are both blessed to have had some of nature's help that night."

"Amazing," Alisha said, remembering how they'd quoted part of Psalm 42 to each other. "He was beautiful," she said, her eyes holding Nathan's. "I hope that big deer stays safe out there. He obviously likes the bird-house path."

Martha spoke up. "I've seen those beautiful bird-houses. We've often wondered who owns that land. Did you say you were hiding in a cabin?"

Alisha's gaze crashed with Nathan's. "Yes."

Nathan looked back and forth between his parents. "I own the cabin. I bought the land and built the cabin even though I don't get to stay there as often as I'd like." He shrugged and lowered his gaze. "And, Mamm, I made the birdhouses."

Martha gasped and reached out a hand to him. "All this time, they brought me such joy and to know they were made by my son. *Denki*, Nathan. That and now knowing you've been nearby all this time. Another gift to cherish."

Nathan held his mother's hand tight but he didn't speak.

Soon, they had the whole story. Amos sat still through all of the chatter. "If I may speak," he said, a gentle tone in his voice.

"Or course, Amos," Mrs. Campton said, her smile beaming.

"I am glad we have our Nathan back. I have prayed toward that end. And I'm happy to share our home with all of you today."

Judy Campton straightened in her chair. "But?"

Amos shook his head. "What makes you think I have more to say?"

"Just a hunch," Mrs. Campton replied, biding her time.

"But there is danger out there. We don't abide by this kind of violence but… As my wife has pointed out, *Gott verlosst die Sein nicht.* God doesn't abandon one of his own so I cannot turn away a loved one in need."

"But you still want us gone, right?" Nathan said, coming to stand by where Alisha sat.

"It's not that I want you gone," Amos replied, his gnarled hand moving down his beard. "I am thankful for your return but I want that evil out there gone."

"We all do," Granny replied. "We all do. We have prayed for that and with the help of Nathan and the authorities, we hope that will come to pass."

Nathan's gaze touched on Alisha. "We have a new plan and we don't want to involve any of you in it," he said. "But that's for another day. Alisha and I need this reprieve. It's been a long time coming."

"We can all agree to that," Amos said, standing. "Martha, *kumm.*"

Nathan's mother motioned them to the table. Nathan and Alisha served the coffee and passed the food, unusual tasks for a man in an Amish house but Alisha appreciated him doing it.

Soon they were passing gifts. Alisha received some knitted gloves from Martha and Nathan was handed a basket full of preserves and jellies.

"I'll keep them here for you," his mother had whispered. "For when you return for home-cooked meals with biscuits and bread."

"That is a plan, Mamm," he told her.

Everyone received a small token and no one complained. Alisha took this simple Christmas morning as an example to use when she returned to her life. If that day ever came.

The day passed too soon and while her grandmother and Mrs. Campton were strong and spry, they needed their rest. So after the early dinner feast was over, Amos offered to take them home before dusk settled.

"It's not safe for you," Bettye said, shaking her head.

"If it was a trip you were willing to make, then I can certainly do the same," Amos retorted. "I will not even need a disguise."

"I'll come with you," Nathan offered. "I can wear a hat and coat and no one will know it's me."

"Do you think that's wise?" Martha asked.

Alisha's heart went into overdrive. "Nathan, maybe we should get word to Josiah? You're injured and can barely use your left arm."

"Josiah said he'd come back if we needed him," Bettye added. "I have my cell with me, just in case."

Nathan lowered his head, thinking. "I shouldn't leave you alone but I don't want Daed going into town by himself."

"Then you should go," Alisha replied. "Josiah knows we'll use the phone booth or Granny's cell to call Raesha's work cell if we need him."

Nathan took her to the side. "I'd feel better taking them back. My *daed* will insist on going so I should go with him. Use the gun I gave you last night if anything happens. We should be there and back in less than an hour."

In the end, Alisha couldn't argue with him. She wanted her grandmother and Mrs. Campton to get home safely. So she hugged them tight and thanked them for taking this risk. Then she stood with Martha and waved goodbye to them, her heart pulled in so many different directions, she wasn't sure she'd ever breathe normally again.

Nathan had made this happen. In the midst of running for their lives, he'd brought her a gift she'd never forget.

Now she just had to worry about Nathan and his father making it back without any problems.

SEVENTEEN

Martha walked up to where Alisha stood by the front window.

Close to an hour had gone by and the snow was falling again in soft, silent flakes. It would be fully dark soon.

"Here," Martha said, holding up a cup of tea. "Meadow tea, mostly mint and sugar but good for calming us down."

"It's getting late," Alisha said, taking the tea, her eyes still on the road. "Thank you, Mrs. Schrock."

"Call me Martha," the other woman said. "We don't stand on formality around here."

Alisha turned away from the window, the last of the sun's feeble rays casting out in a golden sheen over the snowy yard and woods while the snow clouds hovered, waiting for nightfall. "I wanted to thank you for today," she told Martha. "I was so touched by what Nathan did and how you welcomed my grandmother and Mrs. Campton into your home."

"Nathan thought that up and made it happen," Martha explained. "He knew you wanted to be with your *gross-mammi* today." She glanced around. "Judy Campton has always been a friend to the Amish and we all adore your *grossmammi*. It was a pleasure to host them today."

"I so wanted to spend Christmas with her," Alisha replied, sipping the herbal tea, the cup warming her hands, the scent of mint lifting to her nose. "I'll never forget what Nathan's done for me. And not just his kindness today. He has always been a protector."

Martha patted the chair next to her rocking chair. "*Kumm*, Alisha. The food is put away and tomorrow, we'll celebrate again with other family members. Sit and finish your tea. If the men are hungry when they return, we'll allow them a snack."

Alisha's skin felt hot, her nerves on fire with worry for Nathan and his father. This nightmare seemed to go on forever. Tomorrow, they would go back to Philadelphia and get moving on finding a way to end this. She should have done that in the first place but fear and a need to be with her grandmother had held her back. But in her heart, she knew she'd called Nathan that night because she needed him—his strength and his ability to make others feel safe. Admitting that she couldn't do it all alone would have made her feel weak before. But now, she could understand that the hole in her heart could only be filled with the kind of courage love brought. She couldn't live in a spirit of fear and she'd always considered herself fearless. But having Nathan back in her life had shown her how she needed her faith to give her strength. She also needed Nathan—to pour her love out on.

Had could she have let this happen? Falling for him yet again? There could be no good end to that so why did it feel so right?

She sank down next to Martha and put her cup of tea on the table, her hands shaking. "I…want this over."

Martha took up her knitting. "I know you do."

"He's been right there, protecting me all this time."

"You mean, from those horrible men?"

"Yes, and even before then when we had to work some cases together. He always overstepped and somehow tried to help. It was annoying at the time but now I can see so clearly that he wanted to do whatever he could to find that justice we both keep seeking." With a resigned sigh, she added, "And he was watching over me like a guardian."

"Because he still loves you."

"What?" Alisha's head came up, her breath catching in her throat. Did his mother see that she still loved Nathan, too?

"My son loves you," Martha said, her serenity intact, her eyes void of any judgment.

Alisha wanted to tell Martha she might be wrong, but she couldn't breathe. She could very well be having a panic attack.

But before she could break down and confess to Martha that she loved Nathan, too, they heard a noise outside.

"They're home," Alisha said, getting up to race to the window, relief allowing her to take in air again.

Then she saw the vehicle parked near the edge of the woods.

Turning to face Martha, she turned a cold, still calm. "It's someone else. We need to prepare."

Martha went into action. "The barn. Amos told me to run to the barn if anyone came."

"I don't know if we can make it," Alisha replied, searching the front yard. "I don't know how many might be out there."

When they heard a footstep on the broad front porch, Alisha nodded. "The barn has weapons."

Marth bobbed her head. "*Ja*, and it also has animals that will put up a ruckus and give us time to hide."

Rushing to the mudroom, she grabbed two dark cloaks. Shoving one at Alisha, she whispered, "Put this on. It will shield you from the cold and hide you in the dusk."

Alisha put the cloak on and hurried to her room to get Nathan's Beretta. The weapon would also shield her. Because she'd use it to protect Nathan's mother and herself.

Taking Martha's hand, she followed the older woman out the back door then pulled her into the corner Nathan used to hide when he was making calls. After checking the yard and woods, they hurried past the few trees that offered protection and then sprinted toward the front of the big, hulking building. While Alisha watched, Martha unfastened the heavy hinges and motioned Alisha into the big, dark barn. Then she carefully closed the doors and looked into the darkness that engulfed them.

After her eyes adjusted, Alisha spotted a big rake standing against the wall. Grabbing it, she worked to slip it through the inside handles of the doors. "To give us some time," she whispered, taking Martha's hand in hers. "Where should we hide?"

Martha guided her to an empty stall in the far corner where stacked hay stood behind a cluster of feed sacks, milking buckets and hanging harnesses. Crouching, they huddled against the hay behind the feed sacks. The milk cows danced in a restless anxiety, thinking they might be fed or taken care of.

The big draft horses shook out their manes and neighed softly.

Martha had been correct, just as Mrs. Campton had said about the stag in the forest. The animals sensed something was not right.

"They could hear the animals and come to look," she whispered as she and Martha crouched in a corner near the gun cabinet.

Martha adjusted her cape and did a quick peek around a feed sack. "Maybe the nervous animals will scare them away. I heard that happened last night."

So Nathan had told them about that. Remembering their kiss underneath the oak, Alisha wondered if Martha knew more than she'd voiced. That didn't matter right now.

Outside, the goats voiced their own alerts, their displeasure rising in a confused harmony as they bawled and bayed.

"That old male goat doesn't like anyone messing with his female companions," Martha whispered. "He has a pair of painfully sharp horns."

Then the women heard someone trying to get inside the barn upfront. Through the doors.

They'd secured the main doors but not the doors opening to the goat room and pen. "They'll come around and try." Alisha started searching for things to put in front of the back door. She could move a couple feeds bags to trip them, or tie a rope across the doors to slam them back toward the goats.

"They'll get rammed if they enter that goat pen," Martha said with assurance. "The goats will gather around and stall them until we can run."

Alisha thought about that and tried to form a plan that would protect Martha. "We'd have to head to the edge of the woods, near the road. Then I can run to the phone booth."

Wishing she'd grabbed her cell, she listened for footsteps.

They heard the doors jarring again, the pounding and knocking coming quickly this time. With a grunt, someone crashed against the massive, heavy doors. Then Alisha heard the sickening sound of a silenced gun.

"They're trying to shoot the locks off. That won't matter, but the rake won't hold forever," Alisha whispered.

Martha gave her a questioning glance. "We can send out the drafts."

"The horses." Alisha had always admired the sturdy draft horses they used to farm the land. "What if one of your horses gets shot or hurt?"

"Better than one of us getting the same," Martha replied.

They formed a plan. Alisha would pull the rake out of the door handles and allow the man to crash through. Martha would rouse the big drafts and have them waiting and then at the exact same time, she'd send them running.

Hopefully, the animals would knock their intruder right off his feet so they'd be able to get away and also help Alisha and Martha escape. The plan didn't go much further than running to the woods, however.

"On three," Alisha said as they moved slowly toward the doors. The barn had saved them from being assaulted in the house but now, they had one chance to make a run for it.

"If this doesn't work," Alisha said when they approached the heavy doors, "then you run, Martha. Run as fast as you can and I'll deal with whoever this is."

"How can I leave you?" Martha asked, her eyes shining with dread and fear.

Alisha lowered her voice but made sure Martha heard her. "Just do it. I won't have your death on my head, too."

Nathan turned the old buggy into the lane, relieved that they'd gotten Bettye and Judy settled. The two women had insisted they bring home cake and cookies even though they'd barely dented the feast his *mamm* had prepared. He'd gain ten pounds if he stayed here much longer.

"Go and get warm, Daed," he told his father. "I'll put away the buggy and rub down Petunia." The ornery mare lifted her nose and snorted her approval on that.

"*Denki*," Amos replied, nodding as Nathan stopped at the side of the house to let him off.

Nathan clicked the reins and started Petunia toward the barn, but his dad came running to stop him. "Nathan, the front door is open."

Nathan stopped the mare and hopped from the buggy, his heart surging as he sprinted past his father. "Stay by the buggy," he called, using his good arm to wave his father away from the house.

Nathan crashed through the front door, his heart fighting to burst from his chest. What had he been thinking, leaving the women here alone? He'd enjoyed the drive with his father but he'd been concerned about leaving Alisha and his mother here. And for good reason.

Now he hoped he wasn't too late.

After moving through the house to check the dark rooms and finding no one, he sprinted to the back door and out into the yard, careful to stay behind the trees until he could get his bearings. The crescent moon hung low in the sky, causing shadows to cast wide from the woods and the barn. When Nathan felt a hand on his arm, he whirled, ready to fight, and found his father standing there holding a shovel. "Use this if need be."

Nathan let out a breath. "I'm afraid to call out. They'll take them if they know we're here."

His father shot him a grim look, but thankfully, didn't remind him that this was his fault. This couldn't be happening all over again. He wouldn't lose another family member to evil and he would not lose Alisha again—to that same kind of evil.

Then Amos lifted his head. "Listen. Do you hear that?"

Nathan squinted and listened. "The barn? Someone's trying to get in the barn."

Amos rushed past him, but Nathan held him back. "They must have hidden there and now someone is out to find them."

"We must go," Amos said, lifting away.

"You stay. I'll go," Nathan said, a gentle plea in his words.

"Bring your mother back to me," Amos replied, that same plea caught in his words.

Nathan hurried toward the barn but when he was about to make the last sprint toward where a man stood trying to pry the door open, he heard a great swish and watched as someone from inside shoved one of the big doors open. Then the two big drafts came charging out. The surprised man trying to break in screamed and went down, one of the horses hitting him and knocking him over.

Amos rushed forward. "*Was der schinner is letz?*"

His *daed* wanted to know what was wrong. So did Nathan.

They hurried toward the barn but when Nathan saw two caped figures emerging, he let out the breath he'd been holding.

"Daed, it's Mamm and Alisha!"

"Nathan!" Alisha tugged Martha with her as they hurried toward the two men. "Nathan, are you okay?"

He took her in his arms while his father did the same

with his mother. The sight and feel of her alive made him want to never let go. "We're fine. What happened?"

She quickly caught him up. "We had to find a way to escape. We were hiding but he kept trying to get in."

"Stay here." Nathan went over to where the man lay unconscious, bending to check his pulse.

Alisha joined him while Martha stayed close to Amos. "Is he alive?"

"Yes. But he's probably going to be in a lot of pain when he wakes up." The two drafts circled back around and together his parents guided them back to the barn. "I need to call this in and get an ambulance out here."

"So now we'll have two suspects in the hospital."

"Yes, and behind bars after that. If we can hold them long enough to make them talk."

When he stood, Alisha touched his arm. "Nathan, this ends now. Hiding out isn't going to stop this. Tonight was another close call."

Nathan nodded and pointed to the ground. "Yes, too close."

Alisha gasped as she spotted the silencer on the gun the man had been carrying. "I knew he had a silencer. He tried to shoot out the barn door."

"A professional," Nathan said. "He's been watching for days and today, I gave him the perfect opportunity."

"Enough," Alisha said. "I'm leaving here with or without you and I'm going straight to the Philadelphia police and I'm calling the FBI field office to tell them I'm alive and well and ready to tell them what I know. We need to stop running and since that was our next plan and our best plan, I have to cooperate."

Pulling out his phone, Nathan realized he'd failed her yet again. He'd tried to protect her but she'd been close to death several times now. When would he learn he couldn't save anyone on his own? Not his sister and not even Alisha.

He hit numbers, but his heart cried out to God.

As the deer pants for water, so my soul longs for you, O God.

Nathan couldn't do this alone. He needed God with him.

And he needed Alisha with him, too. He'd been denying that for years now.

After calling the authorities, he turned to where Alisha stood shivering in the cold. "The police are on their way with an ambulance. Let's get you inside."

"What about him?" she said, staring over at the man on the ground.

"I'll stay here until they arrive. We shouldn't move him." Then he checked the road. "We need to keep this low-key."

"You might need this," she said, her voice stronger now.

Nathan looked down to where she held his gun against her cloak.

"I didn't fire it," she said. "But I would have."

"I know," he replied. "It's time to get you somewhere safe."

"Yes, a place that won't bring anyone else we love to harm."

EIGHTEEN

Why was going away so hard?

Alisha looked into Martha Schrock's sweet eyes and saw the pain of a mother watching her son leave yet again.

"I don't know how to thank you," she whispered to Martha as they huddled near the door watching for the unmarked car to arrive.

It was early and dawn would be here soon. The whole world glowed white, the snow covering everything like a chenille blanket. The white houses and barns in the distance hulked like weary giants against the sky. The wind held a piercing chill that caused Alisha's tears to slip silently down her cold cheeks.

"No thanks needed or expected," Martha replied, taking Alisha's hands in hers. "No matter what, we have our Nathan back and that is a gift that can't be taken from us." Then she leaned close. "I know you will protect him with all of your heart."

Alisha nodded, unable to speak. Her grandmother and Mrs. Campton had explained this kind of love to her. Men were born protectors but women protected their men with a love that came from the heart—the fiercest kind of love.

Alisha had never truly known that concept until now.

Even when they were young and so in love, she'd been selfish. She'd given up on Nathan too quickly and gone off to do what she thought she needed to do. But she'd become jaded and critical of love, had fought against it and closed off her heart.

She wouldn't do that this time, even if she and Nathan couldn't make it work. But she wanted it to work. "I'll try my best," she managed to say.

Martha hugged her close. "Send word."

Amos didn't hug Alisha but he patted her arm. "*Gott* will watch over you both."

Nathan stood nearby, awkward and clearly shaken. "We'll let you know how things progress."

His mother rushed to hug him. "Take care and Nathan, *kumm* home to see us soon."

"I'll do that, Mamm," he said, his eyes searching Alisha's face while he hugged his mother.

Amos cleared his throat and nodded. Nathan shook his father's hand. "*Denki,* Daed."

Amos didn't speak for a moment but his eyes were gentle on his oldest son. He had not condoned them arriving here but he'd held his thoughts and allowed them to stay. Alisha appreciated that for Nathan's sake. "Better get on."

Carson pulled up close to the house in a plain older-model car.

"Time to go," Nathan said, taking Alisha by the hand. Giving his parents a brief smile, he guided her to the waiting car.

Soon they were huddled in the back seat, warm air taking away the morning chill. Alisha took one last look at the two people standing on the porch.

"Carson?" Nathan asked.

"They put undercover state police all around the property," Carson replied. "You two have kept the town and state police departments busy this Christmas season."

"Thank you," Nathan said.

Carson lifted something from the front seat. "I thought you might want this, Alisha."

"My briefcase," she said with glee. "You got it back."

"After they cleared the cabin, I asked permission to bring it to you. Nathan, your stuff is in there, too."

"Now we have the files we've saved," Alisha said. "Those men were in such a hurry to capture me, they didn't find this."

"We can all rest when this is over," Nathan said, his arm across Alisha's back.

She turned to face him and he gave her a wry little smile. "We'll get through this. I promise."

But that would be a hard promise to keep. If Nathan failed this time, it would be so much worse for him to get over. In saving Alisha, he'd find that redemption he so needed.

She had to work hard to make sure they both stayed alive. After that, she'd figure out the rest. Would he want to stay this close? Or would he go back to being a lonely nomad?

Since they'd left in the middle of the night, Alisha didn't object when Nathan tugged her close. "Sleep," he whispered in her ear. "Rest."

She didn't argue. She might not sleep but she could rest in the safety of his arms. And she said a prayer of thanks for that at least.

When she later woke with a start, Alisha lifted up and stared out at the landscape. "Are we almost there?"

"Hey, sleepy-head," Nathan said, lifting her hair away from her eyes. "Do you feel better?"

"I don't know," she answered, slipping away from his

warm embrace so she could get her bearings. "I've forgotten what better feels like." Then she noticed they were off the main interstate highway into the city. "Where are we?"

"Carson's taking the side roads in a zigzag fashion," Nathan explained. "Better to be safe."

"Not much longer," Carson said over his shoulder. "We're almost to the city."

Sitting back, she watched the buildings and began to recognize the area and then she glanced at Nathan. Since they'd kept on their Amish clothes, he'd put on a dark hat. He was handsome either way, she decided.

To take the edge off the pain that shot through her each time she thought of losing him again, she looked into the rearview mirror. "Deputy Benton, you've gone beyond the duties of a sheriff's deputy. Does Nathan have something on you?"

When both men saw the teasing light in her eyes, they glanced at each other. "He has a lot on me, yes. But I also have a lot on him. We've known each other a long time."

"I've known him for a while myself," she replied, thinking she knew Nathan better now, but she wondered if Nathan ever actually opened up to anyone.

"Is this let's-pick-on-Nathan-time?" he asked, grinning at her.

"Just trying to lighten things," Carson shot back. "Like playing a game of going down memory lane."

"Let's not," Nathan suggested. "We need to be alert."

"Has anyone tried to follow us?" Alisha asked, wishing she didn't have to come back to reality. Delving into Nathan's psyche would be so much more fun.

"So far, so good," Carson said. "I didn't inform anyone outside of the investigating officers about where I'm taking you."

Nathan checked the traffic. "No cars staying on us,"

he said. "I'll be glad when we're sitting in the police station in the middle of the city."

"So will I," Alisha said. "I'd like to mark running for my life off my bucket list."

Nathan took her hand in his, his eyes moving over her. He didn't speak but she knew he had to feel the same way.

Where would things end when they did stop running? What then? They hadn't had time to examine or explore this new kind of normal. Would the adrenaline go away and leave them wishing they hadn't grown so close? Would he regret getting involved with her again?

Nathan's eyes met hers, as if he was having second thoughts, too. "Are you ready for what's next?"

She wanted to tell him she was ready to come out of hiding, not only from these killers, but she wanted to stop hiding her heart and spend the rest of her life with a man she couldn't stop loving.

Instead, she said, "I need to do this so I can get on with my life and feel safe again. So yes, I'm ready."

His expression changed, just a slight shift that went dark for a moment as if a cloud had covered the sun. And then it was gone to be replaced with a blank concern. "Same here. Getting on with my life sounds good."

So he wasn't ready to go all in on their renewed attraction?

Alisha should feel relieved, but all she felt was a deep ache in her heart. He was just biding his time until he could do his duty, find justice and be away from her again.

So she wanted to get on with her life? Nathan wondered if that life would now include him. They'd come a long way in a short time and he wasn't imagining the closeness they'd developed. But he knew being on the run and constantly on guard could mess with a person's head. Going back to normal might cause her to revert back to her old way of wanting to avoid him at all costs.

While he wanted to be with her even more.

"Take us to the station first. We can check into the place I rented later," he told Carson, giving him the directions. "They know me there, but the owner is always discreet and won't give out any information. We can change clothes and freshen up once we've talked to the police."

His phone buzzed as Carson maneuvered through traffic. "The state police." He answered, hoping for good news. "Nathan Craig."

Nathan watched as Carson took another side street toward Belmont Avenue and turned off toward the Philadelphia police department.

"I hate to be the bearer of bad news, Craig," the officer on the other end of the line said. "But the man who was trespassing on your family's property died during surgery this morning. Joe Watson—career criminal with ties to several alleged drug traffickers in the state of Pennsylvania. Mostly opioids, but he's pretty low on the ladder of drug runners."

Nathan inhaled a breath. "So we didn't get anything out of him?"

"He never woke up."

Nathan thanked the officer for the report then told Alisha and Carson. "One tight-lipped and one dead."

Alisha shuddered. "Those draft horses saved our lives but I wish we could have questioned him."

"Yeah, well, onward," he replied after Carson parked the car. "We're about to go into a whole new realm. I know you can hold your own with any LEO. But I'll be there with you."

She nodded. "And Mitchell Henderson should meet us here if all goes as planned."

"So let's do what needs to be done," he said, wishing he knew how she really felt. But like him, Alisha was used to holding her deepest thoughts close.

They walked into the station, Carson acting as body-guard, still dressed in their Amish clothes.

Nathan just hoped the ruse had worked. He now had something more important to take care of other than searching for missing people. Protecting the women he'd loved for most of his life. He only hoped she'd agree to that plan.

Once they'd been put in a conference room, they were given coffee and told to wait. Carson offered to stay, but Nathan shook his head. "You've done enough." Shaking his friend's hand, he said, "Go home and watch over our folks. And watch your back."

"Always," Carson said with a grin. "I'll check in with you later."

"Thank you, Deputy Benton," Alisha said, ever the professional.

She'd removed her *kapp* and shook out her upswept hair. Now her tresses flowed around her shoulders in golden-brown ripples. She looked so young and pretty but her green eyes still held that edge of steel.

Carson bobbed his head. "Anything else you need—just let me know."

After Carson left, they both sat down and went silent.

When had he become so tongue-tied? Nathan wondered.

Looking over at her, he felt the fatigue of the last few days weighing on him like a heavy mantle. "I think I could sleep for a week."

"I had a nap," she replied, her tone tense. "Now I'm wired and ready to get on with this."

"So you'll be done with me?"

Her eyes met his, a silent message that he couldn't read held there in a green forest of doubt.

Before he could answer, a man and woman came in and stood over them.

The man held out his hand. "I'm Detective Jack Mathers and this is Agent Sandy Fenwick from our field office here in Philadelphia."

After handshakes and the usual law enforcement scans and scowls to intimidate them, they all sat down and did another quick back and forth stare session.

Finally, Detective Mathers spoke. "Miss Braxton, you've come face-to-face with some very dangerous people. I'm sorry you had to see that and sorry you felt the need to go into hiding."

"I was running for my life," Alisha said, her voice clear and sharp-edged. "I didn't think things through but I'm here now."

Then the agent leaned forward, her black bob sliding across her cheekbone with a precise swish. "You also got yourself involved in a sting we've been planning for over a year now."

"I didn't get myself involved," Alisha retorted in a touchy tone Nathan knew only too well. "I was in the wrong place at the wrong time and I've been chased, shot at and assaulted since that night."

The detective tapped his pen on the table. "We understand. You should have come in sooner though. This thing goes beyond what you witnessed. Way beyond."

"So you both do understand that she was in a lot of danger?" Nathan replied.

The door opened and a tall man with thick grayish-white hair entered the room, an air of authority about him.

"Alisha," he said, his eyes on her. "I'm sorry I'm late."

"Who are you?" the detective asked, glancing over at the FBI agent and then back to the man.

"I'm Mitchell Henderson, Alisha's boss. Just here to help guide her through the process."

"From Henderson and Perry?" Detective Mathers asked, his expression almost bored.

"The very same," the older man said with a smile that showed practiced grace. "We have firms all over the state and Alisha is a part of our family, so I wanted to check on her. We're all very concerned for her safety."

"Why do you need a lawyer?" Agent Fenwick asked, clearly suspicious.

"Why do you think?" Alisha retorted. "I've got some dangerous people after me and I'm a lawyer for his firm. He's here to protect me and make sure I'm not vulnerable. I might not have made the right decision by running but I'm here now and I know the law."

"But you're not under arrest and we don't suspect you of anything," Detective Mathers pointed out. "Your only crime was not coming back to Philadelphia the night this happened."

"She'd be dead now if she'd done that," Nathan interjected.

"There is no harm in me listening in," Mitchell Henderson replied, his tone firm and polite. "Alisha witnessed a double homicide and she's the only eyewitness. She's here to cooperate and bring these people to justice. I'm here to guide her and advise her."

"Okay then," Agent Fenwick said. "Let's get on with this. Since our two best witnesses are dead now and you witnessed them being assassinated, I'd say we all want the same thing, Miss Braxton. To keep you alive."

"I'd appreciate that," Alisha replied. "PI Craig and I have come up with some notes based on our own investigation. The name Deke Garrison keeps popping up in conjunction with Dr. West. He's high on our list as a possible suspect. We also noted a woman named Andrea Sumter, a patient of Dr. West." Then she told them about the photographer who'd trespassed at the Campton Center. Would you like to compare notes?"

"We don't need to compare notes," Agent Fenwick replied. "We have a solid case but we can't name the suspect yet. We're waiting on more evidence."

Nathan glanced at Alisha and then back to the officials. "You said your two best witnesses are dead now. Are you telling us that this hit was on two people who'd turned state's evidence? The West couple was about to tell all?"

"Yes," Agent Fenwick said, her dark eyes full of aggravation. "They wanted out and we offered them a plea bargain. They agreed but they had to keep playing the part until we could get more evidence. They were scheduled to leave for a holiday trip once they told us everything. They were about to make a fresh start in a new place, under a new name."

Alisha shook her head. "So they *were* involved in criminal activity but they were killed for cooperating with the FBI?"

"That about sums it up," Detective Mathers replied. "We're talking a whole cartel made of several prominent members of society and fueled by low-life criminals who'll do anything for money."

"Why didn't you protect the Wests?" Nathan asked, radars going off in his head.

Agent Fenwick leaned in. "We told them to lie low and we had men on them but they elected to sneak out and do some shopping. So we're glad you decided to share things with us. Because believe me, you're next on the kill list. They don't want you to identify any of their hit men or any of them, and they won't stop until they can silence you permanently."

NINETEEN

Once they'd given their statements, Alisha described the men she'd seen to a sketch artist. When the artist was finished, Alisha nodded her head. "That's definitely the shooter. They called him Ace but he also used the name Adam Baker."

Detective Mathers nodded. "That matches what we have on the official report from the Campton Creek town police." He handed the sketch to one of the lab techs, obviously leaning toward believing Alisha's story. "See if we get a match."

Agent Fenwick grabbed her notes to go off and work her side of the case—mainly trying to figure out if they had enough evidence to bring these criminals to trial. But she stopped at the open door. "All of these details will help and we'll keep after the man we've moved to a nearby hospital. He doesn't have a record other than an outstanding parking ticket. Does a lot of odd jobs here and there so we don't have an accurate work history. Scott Kemp is an alias. He also goes by Scott Kincaid."

Alisha's head came up. "Did you say Kincaid?"

The agent shut the door and came back to the table. "Yes. Ring a bell?"

"It sounds familiar," Alisha said, her gaze hitting on Nathan. "I don't know. Maybe a client?"

Mitchell Henderson had already left for another appointment so they couldn't ask him. Her boss was good at remembering names. "Scott Kincaid," she said, shaking her head. "I know I've heard that name before."

Agent Fenwick waited. "Do you know this man, Miss Braxton?"

Alisha gave her a perplexed stare. "If I knew him, I'd say so. Why do I get the impression that I'm being treated like the criminal here?"

Nathan held up a hand. "Because you ran away, Alisha. You know how this works. You stumbled onto their case and things got blown apart. The agent wants to find closure, so she's leaning on you since you didn't come straight here and put yourself in even more danger. But she's not willing to let us in on exactly who might be targeting us. Probably isn't too happy about the Philly police taking the lead on this, either."

"We can protect witnesses the same as you, PI Craig. Probably better from what we've heard. It is, after all, part of what we do."

Nathan's eyes flared with anger. "Oh, I'm counting on it."

Alisha stood up, putting a hand between them. "I won't have you two trying to one-up each other on my behalf. I ran because I was scared and confused and I wanted to make sure my grandmother was safe. I take full responsibility for not being rational but I gave a complete statement to the officers on the scene and I stand by that. They told me I could go and even offered me an escort."

"They didn't exactly clear that with the FBI," the agent pointed out, her eyes as dark as her hair while she shot a hostile glance toward Detective Mathers. "This whole thing could have been handled differently."

"Beginning with you taking responsibility for keeping your clients from getting shot," Nathan pointed out.

The agent pinned her stern frown back on him. "I have work to do. Since you came in so *we* could help protect you, I suggest you let us take you to our safe house instead of the place Mr. Craig has booked."

Alisha looked at Nathan. "What do you think?"

Nathan studied the detective and then lifted his gaze to the agent. "You *do* have more man power and you *do* want to keep tabs on us, right?"

"That's right. No more taking matters into your own hands."

"I'll consider that," Alisha said. "Right now, I want a hot shower, some food and some clean clothes. That is, if I'm free to go."

Detective Mathers stood up. "Yes, you can go but we'll take you to our safe house in an unmarked car and we'll station officers all around. I suggest you don't try to go it alone anymore, understood?"

"Got it," Nathan said, taking Alisha by the arm. "Let's go and get some rest. I'll keep the reservation at the other place. Just in case."

Both the detective and the agent gave him a bland lift of their eyebrows. "Don't move her again," Detective Mathers said.

After they'd been shoved into the unmarked car, Alisha turned to Nathan. "They have you figured out, I see."

"I don't know what you mean."

"They know you'll go all rogue if things aren't to your liking."

"Well, if I don't agree with how they handle this, yes, I'll do what I have to do."

"I trust you," she admitted. "In fact, I'd say you're the only person I can trust right now."

She wanted to say more but she wouldn't go that far until they had this behind them and could have a fresh start.

That is, if Nathan wanted a fresh start with her.

Late afternoon sunshine moved over what was left of the snow, painting the powdery white trees and sidewalks in shades of vanilla and cream. A leftover wreath on a street lamp hung in limbo, its faded red bows beating helplessly against the wind.

"It's strange being back here," Alisha said as they watched the skyscrapers change into row houses and condos.

Nathan grunted. "I try to avoid cities. Don't like the crowds."

"You could go home," she said, her tone quiet. "You've done more than enough for me."

"Trying to get rid of me now that you have the cavalry behind you?"

"No, just giving you an out."

"I can't turn back now," he replied. Glancing over at Alisha, he looked doubtful. "I don't like relinquishing things to the authorities."

Alisha saw him in a yet another glaringly new light. "Even God?" she asked.

"Even so," he replied, his expression telling her he'd move heaven and earth to protect anyone he loved. "But because of you and God, my parents, your grandmother and Mrs C, I'm learning to trust in Him again, too."

Alisha smiled at that, unshed tears pricking at her eyes. "That's something, I think. Something very important. You've realized the value of family and faith."

His gaze moved over her, a calm in his eyes that told her he'd changed over the last few days. He'd put himself on the line for her and in doing so, he'd come full circle in his faith.

The car pulled up to a quiet street of row houses in a modest part of town. "I'll escort you two to the front door," the patrol officer said. "Then you'll be in the capable hands of one of our best. I'll let her introduce herself."

They were met at the door of the townhouse by a female patrol officer who looked like she'd be able to wrestle a criminal with one arm.

"I'm Officer Milly Sanders," the redhead said with a tight smile. "I'll be with you for the duration."

"The duration?" Nathan asked, clearly not happy.

"Until further notice," Milly explained in slow terms, as if she were talking to a toddler. "Two bedrooms with bullet-proof windows. Don't go near them, however. Two baths and this small living area. I'll take the couch to grab some shut-eye but mostly, I'll be sitting out in the vestibule where I have a clear view of the street."

"Thank you, Officer Sanders," Alisha said, watching as the tall woman lifted her chin and headed to her post.

"Don't try to leave," Milly said over her shoulder. "There's also a guard at the back door into the alley and we've got patrols circling every half hour."

After Milly closed the glass door to the vestibule and took up her position in a folding chair sitting in the small hallway, Nathan turned to Alisha. "It's like they're holding us hostage."

"They're trying to save our lives," she reminded him, her fatigue mirroring what she saw in his expression. "Don't be so grumpy about it."

"They had you in the hot seat back there," he replied

while he paced. "But you did a great job." Finally, he opened the refrigerator and found cold chicken and a fruit salad. "You need to eat."

"And you need to relax," she told him. "I feel better about things now. We were just drifting in the wind out there on our own."

"I guess so," he said, dragging the food out to put on the small counter. Then he located bread and cheese. "I haven't been a very good protector."

"It's a thankless job," Alisha replied as she tore off some chicken and nibbled at the grapes and blueberries. A slow fatigue took over, making her want to curl up and sleep for a long time. But she didn't think a good sleep would ever come to her again.

Nathan handed her some crackers and water then turned to make coffee. "I don't trust anyone here either," he admitted. "The agent perked up when she thought you might know Scott Kincaid."

"I don't know him. I just know the name," Alisha said, grabbing her briefcase. "I'm so glad Carson was able to bring this back to me. Now we can at least have something to do while we stay hidden."

She looked up in time to see the awareness in Nathan's eyes. Did he have other things in mind—holding her close again and maybe kissing her? Officer Milly would frown on that, no doubt.

The moment passed and he said, "Let's see what we can find—after we eat and change clothes."

Alisha looked down at her outfit. "I guess we don't really look Amish anymore."

For a brief moment, she wished she was back at Nathan's childhood home, enjoying the quiet of a cold winter evening, his hand in hers.

But that was just a dream. A silly dream that she could never have even here in the *Englisch* world.

Nathan was tired and so was she. They had to end this horrible nightmare. But ending this could also mean the end of them, too.

After food and a shower, Alisha changed into the jeans and sweatshirt she'd left in her briefcase and Nathan put on some clothes Carson had brought along with the briefcase.

"Our wardrobes are seriously lacking," he said as he padded in socks across the small sparse den, the muted light from one lamp allowing them to see each other.

"But I could get used to living in jeans," she replied. "Feel better after your shower?"

He sure smelled good—clean and fresh with damp hair that couldn't be tamed. She could get used to him, too.

To take her mind away from that, she stared at her laptop screen. "I can't find anything on Scott Kincaid. The name comes up but it's usually someone in another area of the country. No one in Philly as far as I can find."

"It could be another alias…or he's been wiped clean."

"You mean scrubbed from the internet?"

"Yep. It happened. Gone to ground."

"Why?" she asked. "I know he's a criminal but what is it about him?"

"Do you think he could have been the driver that night? Did you hear either of them speak, call out a name?"

"No. They didn't speak. Just pulled up and shot and then left immediately."

"But they watched you so that means they had to be nearby."

"Yes, but the police would have found them on the security tapes by now. I'm sure they hid in plain sight."

Putting down her laptop, Alisha yawned. "I think I'm actually sleepy."

"Then you should rest," he said, his eyes deep-ocean blue. "I'll stay up a while. Give Milly a break."

"Just remember, she called dibs on the couch."

He grinned at that. "Okay, Sugar-bear, go to bed."

Alisha made a face. "You won't let me forget that, will you?"

"I'll never forget it, no."

The silence stretched like an unbreakable wire between them. Alisha wanted to take him in her arms and tell him to rest but she knew that would be crossing the line that pulled at them like a tug-of-war rope.

"Well, good night, Nathan."

He stood and walked her to the door of her room. "How are you, really?"

"What does that mean?"

"I worry about you."

"I'm okay. I'm alive and I'm not giving up."

He held one hand on the door jamb while he kept his eyes fixed on her. "Okay."

Did he want to say more?

"Nathan?"

Touching a hand to her hair, he said, "Get some rest. We don't know what tomorrow will bring."

Alisha certainly understood that concept. So why couldn't he open up to her today?

Nathan heard a thump and then a sharp bang.

Jumping out of bed, he grabbed his gun and went into the den, the moonlight allowing him to do a quick search. Alisha stepped out of the bedroom, still wearing her jeans and sweatshirt.

"Stay behind me," he whispered. "I think we have company."

Alisha nodded and grabbed at his T-shirt, holding tight to the worn fabric.

Nathan moved around corners until he could see into the vestibule. "I don't see Milly."

Alisha shook her head. "I don't either. This isn't good."

Then they heard footsteps and the back door banged open and a dark figure stood looming.

"Run," Nathan said to Alisha. "Toward the front."

He pushed her ahead and fired a shot to give them time to get away, not sure if he'd hit the target or not. Alisha crashed the front door open and let out a gasp. Office Milly lay on unconscious on the floor.

"Nathan?"

"No time. We'll call it in. Right now, we need to get out of here."

They made it out into the yard, the cold snow wetting Nathan's socks as soon as he hit the ground near some shrubs. "Let's follow close to the houses and we'll hide until help arrives."

Alisha did as he said, staying with him as they moved through shrubbery and small entryway gardens until they were at the end of the street. Nathan called 911 and gave the dispatcher their location. Soon, they could hear the sirens off in the distance.

Pulling Alisha close while they waited in a closed storefront doorway, he could feel her shivering. "How did they find us this time?"

"Someone is always watching," she said, her voice shaky. "And we're running out of options."

TWENTY

"I'll take care of everything."

Alisha gave her boss an appreciative smile. "Thank you, Mr. Henderson," she said, too tired to focus on the whirl of the precinct around her.

Dawn had greeted them by the time they'd arrived back at the downtown police headquarters. She should be warm by now since someone had provided her with a blanket and boots. But she couldn't stop shivering. Right now, going to Mitchell Henderson's house seemed like the right thing to do. Warmth and protection and someone else she could trust.

Except Nathan wasn't so keen on the idea.

"Look, we've tried everything," he said. "Something just isn't right. I think you need to be surrounded by a security team day and night and hidden away here at the station."

"I'd have to sleep in a jail cell."

"You'd be safe."

Mitchell Henderson sat down beside them. "I guarantee Alisha's safety, Mr. Craig. My home is gated. No one can get in or out without knowing the code."

"I'm coming with her."

Mitchell didn't even blink. "I'd expect no less."

Detective Mathers came in and slumped into a chair. "Milly has a concussion but she'll be fine. The guard on the back door is still in surgery." Shrugging, he added, "And the intruder got away. No prints. Nothing. I think you're being pursued by some kind of ghost who knows how to shadow people 24/7."

"You think?" Nathan asked, full of fire. "Do you want to tell us who your main suspect is so we can be more aware?"

"I can't do that," the detective replied, his face as blank as the old white blinds on both sides of the room hiding them from the buzz of the precinct and the outside world.

Mitchell stood up. "Look, my staff will take care of Alisha and provide everything she and Mr. Craig need. I've got my own experienced investigators on this, too. None of you have managed to stop this assault. It's time for me to step in and protect my employee. Alisha is a valued member of my law team."

Agent Fenwick came into the room. "Nothing on the intruder. I'm sorry, Miss Braxton."

Nathan looked from her to the detective. "All out of ideas?"

"We're pulling things together," Agent Fenwick replied. "I think I have to agree with Mr. Henderson. But on one condition."

"What's that?" Alisha asked.

"I'm going with you," the female agent said, her dark eyes daring anyone to protest. "I can't let a star witness out of my sight. Last night proved that."

"I agree with her," Detective Mathers said on a drawn-out note full of grudge. "We'll do what we can to help, too. The opioid epidemic is going strong in the state of Pennsylvania but we're so close to nabbing these drug runners. We all want these pill mills gone."

"So, we agree?" Agent Fenwick asked the room in general.

"I'm in," Nathan said. "Where Alisha goes, I go."

"I feel the same, PI Craig," Agent Fenwick replied, her expression closed to discussion.

Mitchell Henderson looked around the room. "Seems I'm going to have a full house for the New Year."

After everyone had left to make arrangements, Nathan glanced at Alisha. "I don't like this. They agreed too readily. I think they know something they aren't telling us."

"Such as?"

"Such as—they know who's after us but they can't say it out loud. They're setting us up as part of a sting. If they mess this up, they'll have me to deal with."

"Why would they let us go to Mitchell's place if they're setting us up?" Alisha asked.

"Maybe he's in on it," Nathan replied. "He seems to keep his cards close to his vest."

"Nathan, we've got to trust someone."

"Like we did last night?"

"These people are relentless," she replied, her tone beyond weary. "If they find us at Mitchell's house, well, then I'll be ready to discuss moving permanently to an undisclosed location."

"Not if they kill you, Alisha."

Later, Alisha stood in the middle of the big bedroom where Mitchell's maid had placed her. "Mrs. Henderson suggested some clothes for you," the dark-haired maid explained with a practiced smile. "Dinner is at six."

"You'll have to thank Mrs. Henderson for me," Alisha said, thinking that had to mean dressing for dinner. But why? She wasn't here to socialize. Remembering Nathan's chilling words to her earlier, Alisha wondered where she'd go from here.

Her silent prayers held her in place. *Lord, let this end in a good way, with justice for those who have died and punishment for those who are evil.*

"Mrs. Henderson is out of town," the maid replied, bringing her out of her prayers. "She sends her regrets but she did instruct me to loan you some clothes."

Funny, Mitchell hadn't mentioned that but Alisha was glad she wouldn't have to indulge Miriam Henderson with idle chit-chat. Miriam was a kind, caring person who lived in her own little bubble of luxury and extravagance. But she'd always been polite to Alisha the few times they'd been at social events.

After the prim maid indicated the closet, Alisha checked and found a couple of wool dresses and some pants and sweaters. She and Miriam were close to the same size. Still, it felt strange to wear these obviously expensive clothes while hiding out.

No matter, she was here now and Nathan was down the hallway. Agent Fenwick had been put in a room between them. Strategy, or to keep her eye on both of them?

Alisha didn't want to delve into that. Nathan was safe and they had an experienced FBI agent on the premises. The Henderson estate had Campton House beat on state-of-the-art security. Gated and back off the street, the big house loomed dark and ominous in the middle of a huge acreage of snow-covered woods.

After going over her notes again, she left her room to go down to dinner. But her appetite disappeared underneath the weight of this stress. Soon it would be a new year. What did that year hold for her?

Nathan called after her. "Alisha?"

She whirled at the top of the spiraling staircase. "Do you have a tracker on me?"

He shook his head. "I heard a door opening."

"Have you seen Fenwick?"

"I'm right behind you," came the edgy feminine voice.

"Do *you* have a tracker on us?" Nathan asked, repeating Alisha's question.

"Should I?" the agent asked, still wearing her dark suit.

"Is it just me, or is this weird?" Alisha asked. "I've been here many times but this feels different. The house is so empty."

Fenwick lifted her eyebrows. "Yes, your boss seems to be thriving here alone and with a skeleton staff. I'm sure he figures the fewer people involved, the better for you."

"He's very dedicated to his associates," Alisha said in Mitchell's defense. "His wife Miriam is out of town. She tends to travel a lot."

"I tend to agree with you there," Agent Fenwick said, her tone and expression neutral. "I did my research on both of them. He's insistent, I'll give him that. His concern for you is touching."

"Why did you agree to this?" Nathan asked, obviously still suspicious.

"I have my reasons, one being I don't want you two out there on some vigilante mission," Fenwick replied, her expression completely blank.

"And you aren't going to share any other reasons with us?" Alisha asked, her gaze meeting Nathan's.

"Need-to-know basis," the agent said as they came to the bottom of the stairs. "Which way is dinner?"

Nathan gave Alisha a warning glance while she led the way to the huge formal dining room. Mitchell was waiting before the roaring fire near the long table. Four places had been set at the end near the fire. Cozy in spite of the opulent scale of the room. Alisha couldn't stop the shivers going down her spine, however. She wanted things to be normal again.

"Sorry we can't open the curtains," he said in greeting. "Best to keep the house closed up."

Nathan did his own sweep of the room and then pulled out Alisha's chair. "How long do you think we'll need to stay here?" he asked Agent Fenwick, who took care of her own chair across the way.

"As long as you're safe and Mr. Henderson doesn't mind us hiding out here, I'd say a while." She glanced from them to Mitchell. "But we're close thanks to your cooperation. We have a man in custody and we've taken Corey Cooper's statement. He's beginning to see the wisdom of telling us what he knows."

"Who is Corey Cooper?" Mitchell asked as he placed prime rib on each plate and passed them around.

Agent Fenwick's gaze hit on Nathan and Alisha. The photographer who'd showed at the Campton Center early on might help them break this case, after all. "Sir, I can't really discuss all of the details of this case with you, you understand. I shouldn't have mentioned that."

"I see," Mitchell replied with a knowing smile. "But *you* should understand that Alisha has given me most of the details already. I just don't recall that particular name."

Nathan took over. "This is an amazing house. What year was it built?"

"Nineteen-forty-five," Mitchell answered as he served the rest of the meal. "It's been in my family for well over seventy years."

The dinner went quickly after that, with stilted small talk. No one lingered over dessert and coffee.

"We should find a place to talk," Agent Fenwick said

as they headed upstairs. "I saw a small den just past your suite, Miss Braxton. Meet there?"

"We'll be waiting," Nathan said.

After she went into her room, he added to Alisha, "I'll check the place for bugs."

"Nathan, stop being so paranoid," Alisha said, her own doubts nagging at her. "We have one of the men who attacked us at the cabin in custody at a hospital nearby and we have Corey Cooper's cooperation now. If he can verify my identification of any of these men, then that's something, right?"

"Right." Nathan guided her into the small den where circular windows highlighted the hills and valleys down past the pool and backyard. But the heavy blinds were shut tonight, the yellow glow of security lights shining against them.

After checking underneath lamps and feeling under the furniture and across the mantle of the small fireplace, he turned back to Alisha. "I've got a bad feeling, Alisha. I don't like this."

"Nathan, stop scaring me," she said, aggravation and exhaustion making her snap. "We're safe here."

"Don't you find it strange that your boss insisted on bringing us here? That he knows a lot about this case?"

"He knows me," she replied. "He's doing the same as you, trying to keep me alive. Do I need to remind you he's had a team on this since the night this all happened?"

"No, I'm well aware of that." Nathan plopped down in a cushioned chair. "I think we need to get out of here."

Agent Fenwick walked in and shut the door. "You aren't going anywhere. It's too dangerous."

"Thank you for being the voice of reason," Alisha said. "Nathan doesn't trust anyone."

"Well, PI Craig, you need to listen to what I'm about

to share with you," Sandy Fenwick said, "and you need to understand that no one else can know this."

"We're listening," Nathan said.

"Alisha, you stumbled onto two of the major players in one of the biggest pill mills in the state of Pennsylvania. All of the people you've found in your searches—the Wests, Deke Garrison and Andrea Sumter—are a part of this highly efficient network. They have mules and runners and spies everywhere. They hire drifters, people who do odd jobs, criminals, you name it. They push Medicare fraud by soliciting legitimate doctors to write fake prescriptions and they give them a cut. That's how the Wests got involved—their greed finally did them in. This pill mill pushes fentanyl like candy and they specialize in everything from oxycodone to heroin."

She took a breath. "We were about to reel them in when this happened. Someone got word and hired this hit. Now they're all scattered to the wind."

"And one of them wants Alisha dead because of what she saw," Nathan said, his expression grim.

"I think they all want her dead," the agent replied. "And I think someone close to Alisha has been tipping them off."

"Do you believe her?" Nathan asked Alisha later after Agent Fenwick had gone to her room. She hadn't told them who she suspected but Nathan had a pretty good idea.

"I can't imagine who would do such a thing. I called you and then Carson got involved. I don't believe the Campton Creek town police would tip anyone off."

"Your grandmother and Mrs. Campton wouldn't knowingly tell anyone your whereabouts."

"No, and neither would your family."

"That leaves one person," Nathan said, hating to voice what his gut had been shouting.

"You can't be serious," Alisha replied. "Mitchell? He's been my mentor for years, Nathan. He promised me a job right out of law school and he's been working night and day to help us."

"I asked you before if you trust him and I can see that you do, but maybe we need to rethink this."

"What does that mean?" she asked, her expression stubborn, her eyes moving toward the big hallway outside the sitting room.

"Scott Kincaid knows something," Nathan replied. "But he won't talk unless we push him."

"Are you suggesting we try to question the man?"

"They did move him closer in to the city so they could watch him."

"I don't know how we can make that possible. We're supposed to stay here."

"Just consider what I'm saying," Nathan replied. "Let me walk you to your door." He stood there wishing he could pull her close and protect her forever. "I'm worried, Alisha. This is all too neat."

Alisha shook her head. "We're both just tired. Get some rest and we'll get back at this tomorrow. Maybe the FBI will get something out of this man."

Nathan could tell she thought he was either imagining things or he was just too suspicious.

But Nathan knew he was on the right track. And that meant he had to get her out of this creepy house.

TWENTY-ONE

Once she was in her room, Alisha pulled out her laptop and did another search of the names Scott Kemp and Scott Kincaid. She'd always been good with retaining information but the constant running for her life had her brain muddled.

So if Scott Kincaid was in the system, why hadn't his name popped up when she'd done her first search? Surely, the firm's investigators had found something other than a speeding ticket on him. Wondering if Mitchell might still be up, she decided she'd go down and ask him.

But she stopped at the door. Nathan didn't trust Mitchell. Could he be right? Alisha didn't want to panic and she didn't want to jump to the wrong conclusion. For as long as she could remember, Mitchell Henderson had been on her side. Why would that change because of this case?

Could he be somehow involved? Agent Fenwick said this pill mill went far and wide, but Mitchell? He and his wife rarely drank anything stronger than wine. She couldn't see him being involved in moving illegal drugs. They went to church, supported local causes and worked hard to fight for their clients. This didn't add up.

Deciding she'd go and talk to him and try to see if any warning bells went off, Alisha slipped out of her room and headed downstairs, her socks padding against the upstairs hardwood floors.

When she hit the marble floor near the stairs she saw a light on down the hallway to the right where Mitchell's study was located. The door was partially open but Mitchell wasn't in the study. Glancing around, Alisha decided she'd take a peek at his desk. What could it hurt?

Slipping past the partially open door, she checked the powder room attached to the study. No one there. Mitchell had to be across the house in the master suite. She'd just look around and see what she could find.

After searching the files on the massive desk, she only discovered legitimate cases. Nothing in the drawers or in the credenza. Nathan had to be grasping at straws.

She was about to go back upstairs when she heard Mitchell's voice coming from the kitchen.

"I don't care what it takes. Keep Kincaid quiet," Mitchell said into the phone, his back turned away from the arched doorway leading from the hallway to the kitchen and breakfast room. "We have to contain this mess."

Kincaid? Alisha gasped and turned to run away but in her haste, she knocked her leg against a hallway table, causing the spindly leg to scrape across the floor.

Sprinting toward the stairs, Alisha dredged up a distant memory. A man had been here at the estate once a few years ago, doing odd jobs. The entire office had been invited here for a picnic. Alisha had walked inside to use the powder room and she'd heard Mitchell talking to the man—right there in the kitchen. And he'd said almost the same thing that day.

"Get it done, Kincaid. We can't let anyone see this mess."

Who had Mitchell been talking about? At the time, she'd figured someone had spilled some food or drink in the immaculate house and Mitchell needed the handyman to clean it up.

But what if it had been something more sinister?

She was halfway up the stairs when she heard him behind her. "Alisha, we need to talk."

Nathan woke with a start. Sleeping wherever he landed tended to make him do that. But this time, he was up and searching for his gun. He'd heard a noise. A door slamming, footsteps moving through the house.

Grabbing his clothes, he hit his knee on the nightstand and moaned. You'd think he'd become less clumsy since this tended to be a normal thing. Hopping on one foot, he managed to get his shoes on. A door downstairs slammed. Then he heard an engine revving.

Rushing out of his room, he saw the cracked door to Agent Fenwick's room. Nathan moved fast and pressed open the door. No one there.

Hurrying toward the stairs, he saw a woman lying at the bottom. Not moving.

Nathan skidded to a stop and went on his knees.

The agent lay on the floor, blood seeping from her head. "Agent Fenwick, can you hear me? What happened?"

The woman on the floor moaned. "He took her. He took Alisha. I tried to stop him but…"

Nathan didn't have to ask who. He knew. "I'm going after them," he said. "I'll call for backup."

"Careful. He's going to kill her. Should have warned you."

Nathan stood up and shouted into his cell, his heart

hitting against his chest with such a crushing beat, he almost passed out.

Why had he let her stay in this house? The FBI had used Alisha as bait to capture the real killer.

Why hadn't he put a chair in front of her bedroom door and sat there all night?

How had this happened?

You failed again. It's your fault.

The voice in his head screamed at him. But the voice in his heart told Nathan to be calm, to trust in the Lord, to pray with all his might. He couldn't lose Alisha now.

He wouldn't let that happen.

So he asked God to please be with him and to guard Alisha until he could find her.

"Scott has aged since I first hired him," Mitchell said in a controlled voice. Shoving Alisha through the snowy woods ahead of him, he kept talking. "You always did have a knack for details. I knew you'd remember sooner or later."

"I didn't recognize him that night at the cabin," Alisha said, hoping to get to the truth at last while she tried to figure out how to escape. Mitchell had hit Fenwick over the head after she'd spotted him dragging Alisha down the stairs. She wasn't sure if Nathan had heard anything.

"You and your PI are tenacious," Mitchell said, jamming the gun against her ribs. "Pity that you decided to stop at the Christmas market that night. What are the odds? My men didn't know who you were."

"Mitchell, help me to understand," she said, her breath coming in gasps as he shoved her down the hillside toward a stream below his property. "Why are you involved in this?"

"Miriam," he said, his tone shaky now. "She has a problem with prescription pain pills. An old injury from her show horse days. She found Dr. Joshua West and... that was that. Addicted to opioids."

Alisha's shock caused her to stop and turn to face him. "Miriam? That's hard to believe."

"Hard to cover up, too," he added, his expression bordering on frantic. "She learned to hide it from everyone, including me."

"But why are you involved in this shooting?" Alisha had to know the truth even if she never lived to tell anyone.

"That's simple, Alisha. I hired this hit. I wanted my wife safe and well but Dr. West kept plying her with the drugs and charging her exorbitant amounts of money. When I heard he and his uppity wife had decided to turn, I was furious."

Alisha's sympathy didn't stop her anger. "So you knew from the beginning? You're the one who's been trying to kill me?"

"No," he said, shoving her forward. "I didn't want to kill you, tried to help protect you but if Kincaid talks, he'll name me as the one who hired him. And...you saw the men. They took it upon themselves to try and find you. Too late, I realized they were trying to silence you to save their own necks. They failed and now they're going to turn on me, too."

Shivering, her socks wet and cold, her feet bruised as they moved over brush and rocks, Alisha shook her head. "Mitchell, why are you doing this now?"

"I don't have any choice," he said, his words chopped and rushed. "Kincaid has been blackmailing me for years and now you know who he is. He'll turn, too, and then with your testimony, everyone will know. The others didn't have anything to do with this hit. They'll kill me if they find out what I did."

The others meaning Deke Garrison and Andrea Sumter and a long line of criminals. "Because they'll see that you know too much."

"Yes. I had to send Miriam away for treatment. I'm so sorry, Alisha, but if I don't do this, they will. I'll make it quick."

"And what about Nathan and Agent Fenwick?"

"They'll be taken care of, sooner or later." Glancing behind him, he said, "They can't know, either. Everyone will believe the hit men found all of you."

Sick to her stomach, Alisha moved forward, too numb to wonder what would happen next. He'd shoot her and dump her in the water while someone else killed Nathan and Agent Fenwick. Probably blame it on an attack from outside, spin it to make people feel for him and his family. If he survived, Nathan would have to watch over his shoulder for the rest of his life.

She wouldn't let that happen. She had to find a way to end this.

Nathan found Mitchell's car near the gates leading to the road, the passenger side door open. Using his cell light, he found footprints in the melting snow headed into the woods.

Soon he was on a path that meandered down, the soft gurgle of flowing water telling him that Henderson was taking Alisha down to a mountain stream. To kill her and leave her.

The whine of sirens up on the road gave him hope. But he couldn't wait for backup. He had to hurry before it was too late. Stumbling in the slush and mud, Nathan kept moving down the hillside, the heavy brush and cold snow blocking him.

When he heard voices a few yards down, he stopped and readied his weapon. Before he could take a step, shots rang out.

Nathan's nerves hummed with a lightning fear. He took off running, sliding in the wet until he righted himself. Then he ran at breakneck speed toward the water.

Alisha had managed to distract Mitchell. "My foot. I think something's cutting my foot." She'd leaned down, moaning and waiting for the man holding her to let go for just a moment.

He did. "Sit if you must," Mitchell said, shoving her onto a jutting rock.

Biding her time, Alisha moved her hand over the icy snow until she felt a firm piece of a broken limb. Then with all the force she could muster, she lifted up and brought the heavy piece of frozen wood down on Mitchell Henderson's head.

He moaned and lifted his gun, shooting into the air. That gave her time to kick him and shove him, forcing him to drop the gun. Scrambling, she dived for it and found it then turned as he lunged toward her.

"Stop, Mitchell! Please stop."

With a roar, he kept coming. So she shot at him.

He fell over at her feet, his hands flailing in the cold creek bed's glistening water. Then he didn't move again.

Nathan came on the scene, the dim light from his phone shining over the woods and stream. "Alisha?"

He prayed, the silent screams inside his head holding him frozen.

"Down here."

Alisha!

"I'm coming." He slipped against the rocks, his knee jamming against a jagged branch. But he made it to the stream and called out her name. "Alisha."

"Here."

Nathan saw her then, sitting on a rock, her head down, her arms close to her chest. She was holding a pistol and staring at the man lying on the water's edge.

"Alisha," he said, falling down on his knees in front of her. "Are you all right?"

She nodded, sniffed. "I shot Mitchell."

Nathan pulled her into his arms. "It's okay. It will be okay."

"See if he's alive."

Nathan let her go and pulled the older man away from the water. "He has a weak pulse but he's alive."

Alisha gulped in a sob. "He's the one, Nathan. He hired the hit men."

"We'll talk about that later," Nathan said, sirens wailing back at the house. "I have to call for help now."

She nodded again, her hand reaching for him. "Where do we go from here?"

Nathan turned and lifted her into his arms and held her tight. "We go home, Alisha. We go home."

New Year's Eve

"How are you feeling, Sugar-bear?"

Alisha tugged at the warm quilt her grandmother had covered her with earlier. "I'm okay, Granny. Really."

"You had a nice nap," Bettye said, concern in her eyes. "No more nightmares."

Alisha thought about the last couple of days. "No. I'm sleeping better."

True to his word, once they'd given their statements and all of the law enforcement people were satisfied that they now had enough evidence to bring down the pill mill for good, Nathan had taken her out of the hospital and brought her here to Campton Creek.

Home. He'd brought her home.

And then he'd left while she was sleeping. That had been two days ago. She didn't know if he was ever coming back.

"We have more food than we'll ever eat," Miss Judy said from her chair in the corner. "Are you hungry, Alisha?"

"No," Alisha replied. "Not right now."

"We can watch the festivities on television tonight if you want," Granny suggested, her gaze meeting Mrs. Campton's.

"Whatever you two want to do."

"You've been through quite an ordeal," Mrs C said. "I'm sure Nathan is out there helping the authorities to wrap up this case."

"Maybe."

There would be a lot more to deal with but for now, Alisha was safe and warm and clean after enjoying a long, hot shower earlier. But still, she shivered.

Granny checked her watch. "Supper time."

"You two eat," Alisha said. "I'll just lie here and snooze."

"Okay then." Granny moved with swift agility toward the kitchen. Mrs C heaved herself into her wheelchair and did the same.

Those two, always conspiring.

The bell dinged, meaning someone was downstairs.

"Alisha, do you mind getting that?"

"Uh, okay." Alisha forced herself up and tugged at the black wool tunic that covered thick plaid leggings.

She went down the stairs and opened the door and stared at the man standing there. The man holding a bouquet of roses and a box of candy.

"It's not Valentine's Day," she said, her heart bursting with joy and fear.

Nathan filled the doorway with fresh air and spice. "No, but it is a good day to celebrate."

She glanced behind her. "If you say so."

"I do," he said. "Can you come with me?"

"I'm not sure. I mean, you left without saying goodbye."

"I had some things to take care of."

She had a feeling the two extremely quiet women in the kitchen were in on this surprise, so she didn't bother telling them where she was going. But she had to ask. "Where are you taking me, Nathan?"

"You'll see."

He guided her across the breezeway and into the main house. When they reached the big sunroom, he stopped. "Happy New Year, Alisha."

Alisha stared in fascination at the twinkling lights someone had strung across the room. A bistro table complete with candles and china sat ready, covered dishes of food centered on a nearby cabinet. Outside, the backyard looked like a fairytale, all white and pristine and glistening.

"Who did all of this?"

"I know people," he said, sitting her down in one of the chairs. After he handed her the flowers, he placed the candy nearby and sat down across from her. "We've never actually had a real date, you know."

Alisha put the flowers on the sideboard and gave him

her full attention. "This after you just walked away two days ago."

Taking her hand, he said, "Yes, this, after I walked away all those years ago. Because now I'm free and clear and so are you. We can finally have a fresh start."

"No, Nathan, we can't."

He looked so crestfallen, her heart regretted her words.

"Why not?"

"You know why. You're out there, putting your life on the line every day and this time, it was because of me."

"We survived and we've help put some nasty people away for a long time." Then he said, "But you're the one with courage here. You saved yourself, over and over."

"You saved me," she said. "Over and over. But how do we get past that and go back to normal? I can't work at Henderson and Perry anymore, even if Mr. Perry is begging me to stay."

"You don't have to," he said, lifting her out of the chair, his hands on her arms. "We can work here, together, Alisha. Put out our own shingle and...live the kind of simple life we both love."

Alisha's pulse quickened. "What are you saying?"

Nathan touched his hand to her chin, his fingers warm. "I'm trying in my clumsy way to ask you to stay here with me and...to marry me. Alisha, please. It took near-death to show me how much I still love you."

"You love me?"

"I do. And... I believe you love me. Don't you?"

She couldn't speak so she just bobbed her head, tears piercing her eyes. "So much."

He pulled her close and kissed her. "So want to partner up? Like forever?"

Alisha thought of so many reasons to say no. But then

she thought of the one reason to say yes. She loved this man. Always. And it was her job to protect his heart. Always.

"I can live with forever," she said, tugging his head down so she could kiss him again. "And working here with you would be amazing and challenging and so perfect."

Clapping sounded through the old house.

Alisha looked inside and saw her grandmother guiding Mrs. Campton's wheelchair toward them. They must have taken the elevator.

"I see you do know people," she said, laughing and crying at the same time. "Special people."

Her grandmother and Mrs. C both laughed and started immediately planning a spring wedding. "We'll invite everyone!"

"We will invite everyone," Nathan said. "My family and yours."

"Together," Alisha replied, her heart healed at last. "Thank you, Nathan, for bringing me home."

"Don't ever leave me," he said, holding her close.

"I'm here to stay."

Alisha knew that in her heart. They were both here to stay.

* * * * *

WE HOPE YOU ENJOYED THIS BOOK!

Love Inspired® SUSPENSE

Uncover the truth in these thrilling stories of faith in the face of crime from Love Inspired Suspense. Discover six new books available every month, wherever books are sold!

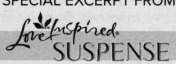
It couldn't be.

Ice filled Ashley Willis's veins despite the spring sunshine streaming through the living room windows of the Bristle Township home in Colorado where she rented a bedroom.

Disbelief cemented her feet to the floor, her gaze riveted to the horrific images on the television screen.

Flames shot out of the two-story building she'd hoped never to see again. Its once bright red awnings were now singed black and the magnificent stained glass windows depicting the image of an angry bull were no more.

She knew that place intimately.

The same place that haunted her nightmares.

The newscaster's words assaulted her. She grabbed on to the back of the faded floral couch for support.

"In a fiery inferno, the posh Burbank restaurant The Matador was consumed by a raging fire in the wee hours of the morning. Firefighters are working diligently to douse the flames. So far there have been no fatalities. However, there has been one critical injury."

Ashley's heart thumped painfully in her chest, reminding her to breathe. Concern for her friend Gregor, the man who had safely spirited her away from the Los Angeles area one frightening night a year and a half ago when she'd witnessed her boss, Maksim Sokolov, kill a man, thrummed through her. She had to know what happened. She had to know if Gregor was the one injured.

She had to know if this had anything to do with her.

"Mrs. Marsh," Ashley called out. "Would you mind if I use your cell phone?"

Her landlady, a widow in her mideighties, appeared in the archway between the living room and kitchen. Her hot-pink tracksuit hung on her stooped shoulders, but it was her bright smile that always tugged at Ashley's heart. The woman was a spitfire, with her blue-gray hair and her kind green eyes behind thick spectacles.

"Of course, dear. It's in my purse." She pointed to the black satchel on the dining room table. "Though you know, as I keep saying, you should get your own cell phone. It's not safe for a young lady to be walking around without any means of calling for help."

They had been over this ground before. Ashley didn't want anything attached to her name.

Or rather, her assumed identity—Jane Thompson.

Don't miss
Secret Mountain Hideout *by Terri Reed,*
available January 2020 wherever
Love Inspired Suspense books and ebooks are sold.

LoveInspired.com